THEODYSSEY

Book 3
Utrophia

I K Dirac

ISBN 978-1-84-327928-0

Cover Design Patrick T Coyne

The Racing House Press
20 Cambridge Drive
London SE12 8AJ, UK
www.racinghouse.co.uk
info@racinghouse.co.uk

Book 3

UTROPHIA

The Theodyssey Trilogy

Book 1. Privateer
Book 2. Libertania
Book 3. Utrophia

1

"Bit tricky that. Don't you agree, Mister Betelgeuse?"

"I do agree, Captain. A most complex set of manoeuvres. It is fortunate that the coordinates we have been given seem to have been accurate, otherwise we might have found ourselves inside the event horizon of one of the black holes, with consequences I need hardly spell out."

Jim had installed himself in his usual position at the rear of the *Bountiful*'s Bridge and was watching the crew as they brought the ship back into 3-space and into orbit around the planet Utrophia. On the large screen, its surface scrolled past. From what he could see, it was mostly arid land with large areas of desert, a number of mountain ranges and only a scattering of what appeared to be vegetation. Its seas were small and its rivers few. As they flew over the dark side, no lights could be seen.

De la Beche stared intently at the screen.

"Any signs of life on this benighted planet?"

"There do not appear to be any urbanisms, Captain," said Mister Betelgeuse. "However, in some areas there are a number of buildings, though they are well separated from each other."

De la Beche continued staring at the screen.

"I suppose we will have to land, but we will need to pick our spot carefully. After what that rascal McGoon said about the reception he received, we do not want to find ourselves assaulted by an army of murderous monks."

Mister Betelgeuse nodded assent.

The ship continued in its orbit, which it completed in just under two hours. Jim watched as Mister Betelgeuse and several other members of the crew studied several screens. Eventually, Mister Betelgeuse spoke.

"Almost all the inhabited areas are on this continent." He pointed to the large screen. "Presumably, because it is the only area of the planet with adequate water supplies. We have selected this area, which is on the outer edge of the inhabited zone, as a possible landing site because our sensors indicate that most of the buildings seem to be abandoned. We should be able to land unnoticed and have time to reconnoitre."

De la Beche seemed surprised.

"Are you sure their sensors won't pick us up as we come in?"

"No, Captain. If you remember, all such technologies are forbidden on this planet."

Just then, one of the crew, whose nickname was Blaster, and who was in charge of the armaments, interrupted.

"I think I'd better tell you, Captain, that all our weapons are out of action."

De la Beche looked at him sternly.

"I don't believe I have given any order to use them."

"Thpat's not what I meant, Captain," came the reply. "We couldn't use them even if we wanted to. They're all out of operation."

De la Beche looked disbelieving. Then Mister Betelgeuse intervened.

"If you remember, Captain, there is very little information available about Utrophia. All we do know is that the original treaty setting it up banned almost all technologies. It appears that there is a force-field around the planet that prevents weapons and similar devices from operating. On the surface, there are no mechanical means of transport. Only pack animals are allowed. The only purpose of the inhabitants is religious observance and adjudication. They are obliged to live pure and simple lives and turn their minds to higher things."

De la Beche pondered this information for several seconds.

"Remind me, darling. What exactly is a pack animal?"

"They are reported to use quadrupeds of some sort to transport loads."

"So it's softly does it, Mister Betelgeuse. You're suggesting we go in on foot, as quietly as possible, keep our heads down, spy out the lie of the land, that sort of thing?"

"That would be my preferred option, Captain."

De la Beche nodded again.

"Right you are, Mister Betelgeuse. Softly, softly, catchee monkey. What about hand weapons? Should we take them in case any mad monks turn nasty?"

Mister Betelgeuse hesitated.

"I'm afraid, Captain, that not only are weapons forbidden on Utrophia, but they probably would not work. If we were found to have them, it might be taken very badly."

De la Beche gave him a baleful look.

"Are you saying that we should go into the lion's den completely unarmed?"

Jim stared intently at Mister Betelgeuse, but could detect no change in his expression.

"I fear we have no choice, Captain, if we are to make any progress in discovering the whereabouts of the Kwokkah. Extracting information by force from those religiously inclined is usually self-defeating. Martyrdom tends to rank highly in their preferred options for demise."

De la Beche sat back in his chair and sighed.

"I suppose you are right as usual, Mister Betelgeuse. That's gods for you. We shall have to look as if we are completely harmless. What about communicators? Surely we can't go without them?"

Mister Betelgeuse nodded almost imperceptibly.

"There is evidence from our scanning that communicators may not work in some areas where there are buildings. I suspect also that any technology would be treated with suspicion. I have taken the liberty of disguising some communicators so that they look like books of prayer. If you press rapidly twice on the symbol on the cover, it will open to reveal the communicator interface."

De la Beche clapped his hands in pleasure.

"Splendid, Mister Betelgeuse! I knew I could rely on you. Now, to put anyone we meet at ease, I shall wear something ecclesiastical. I have just the outfit in mind. You and I will go, of course, Mister Betelgeuse, and Sawbones," he said, turning to Doctor Culpepper, "you had better come along. You never know. We may need your services. And where's Jim?" he said, looking around. "Ah, there you are, Jim. I think you should come too. You seem to be our lucky charm. Where would we be now if all those things hadn't happened to you?"

***

As the cutter came in low to their chosen landing spot, Jim studied the screen. The area did indeed seem to be abandoned. There were a few small piles of rubble that looked as if they might once have been buildings. Remnants of a stone wall ran for several hundred metres. Markings on the land suggested that it had been cultivated and some low vegetation might be crops. In the distance was what appeared to be a larger building, although it was too far away for him to see whether it, too, was derelict.

The cutter pilot scrutinized the sensor screen.

"Nothing animate within five hundred metres, Captain. You should be safe to disembark."

"Thank you, darling. What about that?" said de la Beche, indicating what Jim had thought was a building. "Anything in there?"

The pilot shook his head.

"Nothing indicated, but it's at the limit of the sensor's range. If it's a building with thick walls then anything inside probably wouldn't show up."

De la Beche gestured for the gangplank to be lowered and the company stepped down to the planet's surface. A reddish sun hung low in the grey sky. Jim shivered slightly in the chilly air and watched as de la Beche swept down the gangplank in what he had described as "something ecclesiastical". He wore a long white robe over which was draped a red and green velvet cover, richly decorated with a host of motifs and symbols. Shiny leather shoes with gold buckles peeked out from under the robe, and on his head was a wide-brimmed purple hat.

The ground was covered sparsely with brownish grass and a few low, prickly bushes. Jim listened carefully, but heard nothing, not even birds or animals. The only sound came with the occasional gust of wind. De la Beche surveyed the scene and pointed to the building in the distance.

"The only thing of interest seems to be that pile over there. I suggest we move a bit closer and see if we can find out what it might be."

They moved cautiously, keeping in the shadow of the wall. As they came closer, Jim could see that the building had brown stone walls and a grey slate roof. Arched windows appeared to be glazed with coloured glass. Along one side ran a covered walk-way flanked by columns. Suddenly, de la Beche motioned them to stop and pointed. In the gloom, Jim saw three robed figures pacing slowly along the walkway, heads bowing rhythmically. They reached the end, turned, and then disappeared. A few moments later, he noticed a light flicker in a window.

"They didn't look too threatening," said de la Beche. "I think we might try to make their acquaintance. Sawbones, you and Mister Betelgeuse stay here, just in case anything happens. Jim, you come with me. Your fresh-faced innocence might disarm them."

As they rounded the end of the building they were faced with a large wooden door, studded with rivets, with an iron-ringed handle on one side. De la Beche rapped on it three times with his fist. For several seconds there was no sound. Then the handle turned and the door slowly opened to reveal a hooded figure. Jim saw, beneath the hood, a lined face, a bald pate with wisps of greying hair around the ears and a long, grey beard. The figure stared mournfully for few moments at the resplendently robed and behatted de la Beche.

"From the Inquisition, I presume?"

De la Beche smiled.

"Not at all, darling. I don't know whom you were expecting. We are just making a few enquiries. We were hoping you might be able to help us find something that some friends of ours have lost."

The hooded one's expression did not change.

"Are you sure you are not from the Inquisition? We always expect the Inquisition, you know."

"Absolutely sure. I've never heard of this Inquisition that you talk about. We are here, as I said, in a spirit of friendly enquiry."

Still the mournful expression did not change.

"If you are not from the Inquisition, are you on a pilgrimage?"

De la Beche was momentarily lost for words.

"A pilgrimage?"

The hooded one sighed.

"Are you on a journey seeking enlightenment?"

De la Beche beamed.

"Absolutely. I couldn't have put it better myself."

The hooded one sighed again.

"In that case, you had better come in. It is our rule to offer food and shelter to pilgrims."

They entered a room with white, plastered walls, its windows and doors edged with grey stone. In the middle was a heavy, carved wooden table and several chairs. The figure suggested that they sit down, and made a slight bow.

"Welcome, pilgrims, to our humble abbey. I am Bon August, prelate of our order. We call ourselves the Bonhumes." He clapped his hands and a few seconds later another hooded figure appeared. "This is Credent Guilham. He will serve you. Our fare is simple but good. We have bread and cheese that we make ourselves and a broth made from vegetables grown in our garden. Are you ready for a repast?"

Jim realized that he was hungry. He looked at de la Beche, who nodded.

"Most kind of you, darling."

Credent Guilham left the room. He came back in a few minutes carrying a tray with the food. He was followed by another hooded figure carrying a pitcher and two pottery cups that he placed in front of them, pouring a red liquid from the pitcher.

"Wine from our own vines," said Bon August. "Particularly refreshing for the weary pilgrim."

De la Beche picked up a cup and sniffed it several times before taking a small sip. Jim thought he noticed a slight twitch of the nose before he spoke.

"Most piquant. It is a rather young wine. I fancy it will improve with age."

Jim tasted the wine. It had a sharp, rather bitter taste, but he found it went reasonably well with the bread and cheese. Just as they were finishing their meal, Bon August spoke again.

"All that we ask of pilgrims for their food and shelter is that they join us in our ceremony, the Volumentum."

Jim saw de la Beche's eyebrows rise slightly before he replied.

"Of course, darling. Happy to oblige, though I'm afraid I'm not altogether familiar with your ceremony. What would you like us to do?"

Bon August pointed to a metal object on the wall that to Jim looked like two crosses entwined by what might be a rope, or possibly a snake.

"We believe in the Gods of Good and Evil. The Good God is the god of Heaven, of everything that is light. The Evil God is the god of the earth and of all material things. He has entrapped us in this material prison, but he has no power over the soul, so, by leading a pure and good life, our soul may escape his snares and return to Heaven. The Volumentum is a ceremony of purification. We present to the Good God the fruits of our labours, the sacred scripts that we have copied and adorned from those left by the Ancients. In that way we hope to achieve our heavenly goal and keep at bay the Inquisition, the agents of the Evil God."

"Most commendable, darling, if I may say so," said de la Beche, nodding gravely. "The very best of luck in your endeavours. It's always refreshing to see someone spurning material things. So very rare these days."

Bon August gave a slight nod in response.

"Now, if you will accompany me, the Volumentum can begin."

They were taken into an adjoining room. It, too, had plain, white, plastered walls. At one end was a simple stone altar and on the wall above a larger version of the cross and snake symbol. A procession of hooded figures emerged from a side door. Each was carrying what looked to Jim like a scroll. They sang a simple, repetitive plainchant as they moved towards the altar and placed their scrolls upon it. They stepped back from the altar and lay prostrate on the ground for several minutes, all the time singing the same chant. Then, in unison, they rose to their feet, bowed deeply to the altar, and processed out through the door from which they had entered.

Jim turned towards Bon August and saw he was still bowing. Eventually he stood upright.

"A most moving service, don't you agree?"

"Absolutely," said de la Beche. "Brings a lump to the throat. If I may ask, what is on those scrolls?"

"They are the words handed down by the Ancients that we copy faithfully and decorate with the most beautiful illustrations."

"The Ancients?"

"The founders of our faith. They who have gone before us and have ascended into Heaven."

"Really? What are those words?"

Bon August shook his head.

"I do not know. We cannot read them."

De la Beche looked astonished.

"What do you mean, you cannot read them? You have just said that you copied them."

Bon August's expression took on an even more doleful cast.

"We copy them, but we do not read them."

"Reading can be tiresome, I do so agree. I do as little as possible myself. But I would have thought that it would be – how can I put it? – helpful for you to read something being copied?"

Bon August sighed.

"Once the Ancients had written, there was no more to write and no need for us to read. Our duty is to copy."

De la Beche nodded sympathetically.

"I do see your point, but Jim, here, is a very good reader – and a writer to boot. I expect he could help if you want to know what is written on those scrolls."

Bon August looked doubtful.

"Perhaps we are not worthy to read them. Perhaps we will only know them when we reach Heaven."

"Oh, I think you may be being too modest. I'm no expert in these matters, of course, but, from what I've heard, reading would not be high on the list of priorities in Heaven. There's a lot to enjoy in Paradise, so I've been told."

Bon August's head dropped slightly and he became silent. Jim saw his lips moving, as if he was saying something to himself, perhaps praying. Eventually, he spoke.

"We are instructed to learn from pilgrims as well as offer them hospitality. If you would like to see our scrolls, I will take you to the Scriptorium."

They were led down a long corridor and through a door that opened into a large, high-vaulted room. At two rows of desks sat hooded figures crouched over sheaths of parchment. Most had what Jim thought were pens in their hands, which they dipped periodically into wells let into the desks. A few held brushes and appeared to be painting.

De la Beche surveyed the scene approvingly.

"All hard at it, I see. I'm envious, darling. You must tell me how you do it."

Bon August extended his arm.

"These are all Credents of our community. When they have studied our faith and reached proficiency in the writing and illustration of scrolls, then they may be initiated into the elect that we call Bon."

"Treat 'em mean and keep 'em keen, eh? That's the way to do it. What are they working on at the moment?"

Bon August pointed to the nearest desk.

"This is a particularly important scroll. Credent Jocken is one of our best illustrators."

Jim gazed down at the desk. The parchment was a rich cream colour. A column of text ran down the middle; on each side were illustrations of people and fantastical animals, as well as landscapes and buildings. He tried to read the text, but it was in a curious font, full of curlicues and serifs that made reading diffi-cult. After a while, he managed to decipher the first few lines and read them out:

Utrophia, more properly the *Sacrodominium of Utrophia*, is an
independent planet, the seat of the *High Consistory*, established
by the *Peace of Eridanus* and the subsequent *Treaty of
Opiuchus* that ended the *Thousand Years War*, also known as
the *Wars of Religions*.

On listening to Jim, de la Beche began to study the scroll.

"This is rather interesting. You say the original was left by the Ancients. Is it here?"

Bon August's mournful expression returned.

"It is said that the Inquisition took all the sacred texts left by the Ancients, but we had a secret store of scrolls that they did not find. We copy from them."

De la Beche made a sympathetic sound and asked Jim to continue. Jim found he was beginning to get to grips with the peculiarities of the script and deciphering was becoming a little easier. He read out more:

The origins of the wars lay in the decay and fragmentation of
the *Holy Andromedan Empire*, a loose confederation of planets
that at its zenith encompassed much of the Galaxy. The Empire
was originally bound together by its dominant religion,
Asimatism, which in its final days could be described as an
ecumenical monotheism. It is thought to have developed from
forms of star worship, which isolated societies that have
reverted to primitivism sometimes adopt.

"Most interesting," said de la Beche. "I don't think I've come across anything quite like it before. I think we may need a second opinion. Two of our companions are waiting outside for us. Would you mind if they came in and joined us?"

Bon August seemed surprised.

"Are they also pilgrims?"

"Absolutely, darling. Always in search of enlightenment."

"Then we must offer them hospitality, too."

De la Beche told Jim to fetch Doctor Culpepper and Mr Betelgeuse. As Jim left the abbey, he noticed that a soft rain had begun to fall. He found Culpepper and Betelgeuse attempting to shelter in the lee of a wall. Mister Betelgeuse was as impassive as ever, but Doctor Culpepper looked distinctly morose. The three made their way back swiftly to the abbey. As they entered the Scriptorium, Bon August bowed in welcome and began to suggest that they might like to eat, but de la Beche intervened.

"Time for that in a minute, darling. I would just like to get the opinion of my colleague, Mister Betelgeuse, on this intriguing manuscript. Jim, if you will, read on."

Jim started at the beginning and found that he was beginning to be able to read with some fluency.

Utrophia, more properly the *Sacrodominium of Utrophia*, is an independent planet, the seat of the *High Consistory*, established by the *Peace of Eridanus* and the subsequent *Treaty of Opiuchus* that ended the *Thousand Years War*, also known as the *Wars of Religions*.

The origins of the wars lay in the decay and fragmentation of the *Holy Andromedan Empire*, a loose confederation of planets that at its zenith encompassed much of the Galaxy. The Empire was originally bound together by its dominant religion, *Asimatism*, which in its final days could be described as an ecumenical monotheism. It is thought to have developed from forms of star worship, which isolated societies that have reverted to primitivism sometimes adopt. It postulated a deity that had created the Universe and sometimes intervened in ways that were supposedly benign, but were often obscure and difficult to interpret. It had a very large and hierarchical clerical establishment that presided over elaborate rituals in grand and lavishly-decorated basilicas and that often colluded with ruling elements of society in adjusting doctrine and morality.

Several factors contributed to the outbreak of the wars. First, a succession of weak rulers of the Empire led to many regional leaders operating as local rulers, virtually independently of the Empire, and in some cases threatening secession. Secondly, the vast wealth of the religious establishment and its identification with the ruling classes created enormous resentment among the lower classes and led to frequent and bloody clashes, known as *Peasants' Revolts*. Thirdly, and perhaps most importantly, was dissatisfaction with *Asimatism*. Its god was distant and unknowable. It lacked personal connection with the individual, yet it claimed to be the arbiter of all moral and spiritual questions and to be the sole judge of who deserved entry to the afterlife.

In reaction, on many planets there appeared individuals, often called prophets or seers or magi, who claimed direct communication with a deity and who produced scripts that they said were revelations from their god. These scripts contained detailed instructions on most aspects of life, including moral guidelines, social codes and dietary and hygiene injunctions. They also gave detailed descriptions of the afterlife to which the faithful adherent could look forward. These gods were usually ferocious in their punishment of any who failed to follow the instructions strictly or any who challenged their authority. The very specificity of the codes, and the impossibility of adhering to them completely, proved enormously attractive and resulted in revelatory monotheisms proliferating across much of the Galaxy.

Jim had read the scroll with mounting fascination. He realized for the first time that there was something called history. There was a chronology to events. One followed upon another. One was contingent upon another. The universe was not simply a collection of random, unconnected happenings.

De la Beche looked quizzically at Mister Betelgeuse.

"What are we supposed to make of this?"

Mister Betelgeuse hesitated. Jim fancied he saw an indrawing of breath.

"The style is very much what one would expect of *Galactopedia*, Captain, but the currently available version contains no references to the early history of the Galaxy or, as far as I am aware, to religious conflicts. The *Principia Ontologica* does have some such references, but its veracity is open to question and, of course, its style is very different."

De la Beche turned to Doctor Culpepper.

"What do you make of it, Sawbones?"

Culpepper grimaced.

"It is intriguing, but I'm afraid history isn't my strong suit – nor is religion, really. I see there's more. Why don't we read on? Perhaps that will enlighten us."

De la Beche nodded and Jim continued.

These religions were readily coopted by individual rulers and warlords to justify any action they might take as promoting the true word of God. This proved particularly useful in appropriating the wealth of the old, and hence heretical, religion of Asimatism.

Often the teachings of these religions were diametrically opposed to each other, which exacerbated any clash between them, as each could claim divine inspiration. Wars became frequent and prolonged and were difficult to end, because neither side would recognize the beliefs of the other. On some planets, over ninety percent of the population perished, either directly from warfare or because of the starvation and disease that resulted.

Financial and material exhaustion finally brought to an end a millennium of internecine warfare. An armistice, the Peace of Eridanus, was followed by the Treaty of Opiuchus. The treaty had three main elements:

- The Holy Andromedan Empire was abolished and the various combinations and alliances that had emerged during the years of warfare were recognized as legitimate self-governing entities with mutually recognized boundaries. Any proposed change to these boundaries must initially be by negotiation. If negotiations failed, any resort to conflict must be made by a formal, legal declaration of war and such wars must be conducted in accordance with agreed conventions that were appended to the treaty.

- The principle of *cuius regio, eius religio*, the right of rulers to require all within their domain to conform to the religion of the rulers, was recognized as applicable in all jurisdictions. Exceptions could be made for established religious minorities, but only if they paid additional taxes and acknowledged the sovereignty of the dominant religion.

- To adjudicate on all questions relating to theological, scholastic or other religious matters, a supreme court, the *High Consistory*, was established. All recognized religions would be represented on the Consistory. Its rulings would be final and without appeal. In order to safeguard its independence, it would be established on its own planet, *Utrophia*, which was designated a *Sacrodominium*, or holy domain. Its location was secret and known only to specified religious authorities in each jurisdiction. Only those deputed by such authorities would be allowed to reside on Utrophia. To date, 1436 questions have been submitted for adjudication. No rulings have yet been issued.

De la Beche surveyed the company.
"Are we any the wiser?"

"I did not understand much of what was said, and what I did understand made me uneasy," said Bon August. "Perhaps it was just as well that we could not read it." Doctor Culpepper shrugged, but Mister Betelgeuse continued to examine the manuscript.

"We cannot be sure, of course, Captain, but this document might be referring to real events. At the very least, it does give a plausible explanation for the existence of Utrophia."

"That's a good point, Sechy," said Culpepper. "Who knew what Utrophia was for or where it was or even if it actually existed? I thought of it as a place full of madmen shouting damnation at each other."

"I rather agree," said de la Beche. "If I gave it any thought at all, I imagined Utrophia was just a hell for all seasons." He turned to Bon August. "Perhaps some of these other scrolls could shed more light? Would you mind if we took a look at them?"

"If you must," said Bon August. "We cannot refuse a pilgrim's request, but I am not sure that we would want to hear what they say. Perhaps it is best that the words of the Ancients remain hidden from us."

He motioned to a Credent. Jim watched as the Credent went to a large cupboard with ornately-carved doors, bowed deeply and intoned some words that he could not catch. The Credent opened the cupboard, took out an armful of scrolls and placed them reverently upon a table. Bon August indicated that Jim could begin reading.

The first scroll he read was a treaty between two obscure administrations concerning a planet whose inhabitants objected strongly to being ruled by either. It detailed the nature and degree of the force to be used and the division of the spoils. The next was a description of the wedding of the daughter of the Aurigan Emperor to the son of the Basileuk of Cetus. The celebrations lasted ten days and nights. There were detailed lists of all balls and festivities, of all animals slaughtered and cooked, of all sweets and beverages prepared and served, of all speeches made and of all illicit couplings. Among the other scrolls were the financial accounts of the Polytelian Corporation, which specialized in supplying luxury goods to the flamboyant rich of the Galaxy, and the medical notes of physicians attempting to cure an unnamed grandee of a condition brought on by an over-indulgent and dissolute lifestyle.

"I'm not sure this is getting us anywhere," said de la Beche, as Jim read details of a particularly gruesome medical procedure. Then Jim began reading another scroll:

The High Consistory of the Sacrodominium of Utrophia

Report of Secretary Uraneous Syngrafeas

Under the Treaty of Opiuchus, I have been appointed as Secretary to the inaugural assembly of the High Consistory of the Sacrodominium of Utrophia. Accordingly, invitations have been sent out to all recognized religious bodies in all jurisdictions signatory to the Treaty to nominate members of the High Consistory. All Nominations have now been received and members and their attendants are now resident on Utrophia. However, it has not yet been possible to convene the High Consistory, because almost all members have so far refused to participate. The reasons for refusal include:

- Monotheists cannot be in the presence of polytheists, whom they regard as licentious idolators. Conversely, polytheists cannot sit with monotheists, whom they regard as dogmatic prigs.

- Some claim that they are forbidden to commune with members of other beliefs, except by courier carrying written messages.

- Others claim that they become nauseous in the presence of those whom they regard as infidels, blasphemers or heretics.

- One representative refuses to sit down with those who eat warm-blooded animals that have forward pointing ears.

- The representative of the Cepheid Confederation cannot be in the company of the representative of the Lacertan Empire because the Lacertan foundation myth involves the sodomizing of the god Lykkelig by the god Tordenkrat, from which union the mother of all Lacertans was born. According to the Cepheids, this is not only anatomically impossible, but implies that all Lacertans are in a permanent state of sin.

My Secretariat is engaged in discussion with all representatives on holding the inaugural assembly of the High Consistory. No date has yet been agreed.

There were a few moments silence, once Jim finished reading. "What do we make of this?" asked de la Beche.

"That's god-botherers for you. All the same, if you ask me. Never agree about anything," said Doctor Culpepper.

"I rather agree," said de la Beche. "What about you, Mister Betelgeuse? Have you any observations to make?"

"Well, Captain, this is evidence that supports the first scroll, which suggested that Utrophia was founded for a purpose, whether or not it ever fulfilled that purpose. I assume the original of this was written some time ago. I am beginning to suspect that these are elements of *Galactopedia* that are no longer available from normal sources."

"Are you saying that they have been suppressed in some way?"

"I cannot say, Captain."

"Who would want these things to be hidden?" said Doctor Culpepper. "It doesn't seem to make sense."

"I cannot answer that either, Doctor, but the origins and purpose of Utrophia have always been shrouded in mystery. These documents do at least suggest answers to some of the questions. One very significant question does remain. Do we have any indication as to whether the High Consistory was ever convened? Perhaps Bon August could enlighten us?"

Bon August shook his head.

"I have heard that the Ancients talked of the High Consistory, but I did not know what those words meant. There are other sects and orders on Utrophia. Perhaps you could ask them. We are a poor and simple order. Our mission is to copy the scrolls faithfully. That way we may achieve Heaven."

"Good luck with that, darling," said de la Beche, nodding sympathetically. "I see you have a number of other scrolls that we haven't looked at. I don't wish to take up more of your time. Would you mind if I took a snap of them. Then Jim could read them later."

Bon August looked puzzled.

"What is a snap?"

"It's just taking a picture of them. It will only take a second or two, and it won't harm them."

Bon August assented.

"Our mission is to serve pilgrims."

De la Beche smiled in appreciation.

"We have a mission, too. Have you ever heard of the Holy Kwokkah?"

Bon August shook his head.

"No. What is it?"

"It is a vessel, we think, sacred to those who live on the planet Nullarbor. Do you know of them?"

Again, a shake of the head.

"No, but a vessel, you say. Are you on a Grail quest?"

This time, it was de la Beche's turn to be puzzled.

"A Grail quest?"

"Yes," replied Bon August. "We call a sacred vessel a Grail. If it is a Grail you seek, then perhaps you should enlist the aid of the Knights."

"The Knights?"

"Yes, the Knights of the Sacred Circle. Holy warriors. Their mission is to seek Grails."

De la Beche looked at him quizzically.

"Let me get this straight, darling. Are you saying these Knights go round looking for things you call Grails?"

"Yes. It is one of their holy missions."

"Most interesting. Do they ever find them?"

There was a long pause before Bon August replied.

"You must ask them, but it is said that the whole point of a Grail quest is that the questing is all."

"Questing is definitely not all for us," said de la Beche. "However, it might be useful to have a word with your Knights. How do we find them?"

"You cannot find them," replied Bon August. "They must find you."

"How can they find us, darling? They would have no idea that we are here."

Jim thought he saw a trace of a smile on Bon August's face.

"Their ways are mysterious. We will pray and perhaps you will meet."

De la Beche gave a nod of appreciation.

"Most kind of you, darling. Every little helps."

Jim watched as Bon August bowed his head and closed his eyes. He stood for several minutes, lips moving soundlessly. Eventually he reopened his eyes.

"Our prayers have been answered. I will send them a signal. They will meet you."

2

Sloakum surveyed the bleak landscape of Utrophia from the bridge of the *Rum, Sodomy and the Lash*. He did not like what he saw one little bit.

"I seen prettier rats' arses, Maggie. Fancypants ain't gonna stay there more'n five minutes, ye can bet on that. Not him and his lah-di-dah ways. He'll be long gone."

Maggie gave him a withering look.

"Ye always were a lazy bilge-sucker, Jonah Sloakum. Ye just don't want to bestir yerself and look for him, That's the be all and end all of it. He'll be there, ye mark my words. Now, let's get after him. Do we know where he went down?"

She looked contemptuously at the ship's comms operator, Long Tom Tapper, named for the sound his wooden leg made as he moved, who was slumped over a terminal. She grabbed his ponytail and jerked his head upwards.

"This pox-riddled cur is stewed again. I ain't never seen a gizzard more fit for slittin'. What are ye waiting for, Jonah Sloakum?"

Sloakum looked down shamefacedly and mumbled.

"I ain't got no one else as can do that work, Maggie. We'll have to wait till we're next ashore. He'll come round if ye slap him about a bit, maybe throw a bit of water on him."

Maggie walloped Tapper's face several times, before fetching a bucket of water and pouring it over him, much to the amusement of the rest of the crew. Tapper groaned and showed signs of stirring.

"Wake up, ye useless bag o' grot, or I'll have yer shrivelled gonads fried and fed to the ship's cat."

Tapper groaned again and his eyes opened. Maggie thrust her face into his.

"Have ye any idea where Fancypants de la Beche might have set his pomaded arse down in this hellhole?"

Tapper swayed back and forth, his eyes crossing as he tried unsuccessfully to focus on the sight before him. Maggie slapped him several more times and a few words emerged as he gestured unsteadily with his right arm.

"Down there ... we got signals ... or something like that."

Maggie slapped him again.

"Whaddya mean, something like signals?"

Tapper waved his arm again in the direction of a large screen. "Down there. That's where he might be."

The screen showed a particularly unappealing part of the Utrophian landscape. All Maggie could see was bare land dotted with scrub and what might, or might not, be a few buildings.

"Why'd he want to go there?"

Tapper gazed back at her blankly.

"Signals ... signals say..." He slumped down again.

Maggie gave him a kick that sent him sliding across the floor, still unconscious. She looked at Sloakum, shaking her head.

"Is that the best we can get from this bunch of scurvy scumbags ye call a crew, Jonah Sloakum?"

Sloakum shrugged.

"I'll string a few up for ye next time we're ashore, Maggie, if it'll make ye happy, but we'll have to make do with what we've got fer now."

Maggie shook her head sadly.

"Ye're gettin' soft in yer old age, Jonah Sloakum, like all men. No use, the lot of ye. I suppose we'll have to go down there. Someone told me they don't allow females down there. We'll see about that. I'm better than any man or any of you bunch of bilge rats. Anyone going to argue?" No sound came from the crew, most of whom kept their heads down. "It'll have to be you, me and Dick McGoon. He's been there before, so he might be of some use fer once."

McGoon was looking at the screen. He gave a start and protested loudly.

"Not me, Maggie. I know that place. It's all coming back to me now. That's where we landed last time and we was nearly done fer. I've been once and it was more than enough fer me. I ain't going back fer no one."

On hearing McGoon, Sloakum took a sudden interest.

"Ye said ye landed there because ye thought there was all sorts of gold and treasure there. Is that right?"

McGoon answered warily.

"Maybe, but we never came near to getting our hands on any."

At the mention of gold and treasure, Sloakum's enthusiasm began rising.

"Maybe we need to go and have a little look see. Help ourselves to a bit of what's there."

McGoon's fear rose further.

"Ye wouldn't say that if ye'd seen what I seen."

Maggie glared at him, legs akimbo, arms on her hips.

"I always knew ye had rat's piss fer blood, Dick McGoon. I could never be sweet on the likes of milksops. Is that what ye want me to know ye as?"

McGoon answered in a low, whining voice.

"I ain't no milksop, Maggie. Ye know that."

Maggie was unmoved. She gave him another contemptuous look.

"Prove it then, Dick McGoon. Prove ye're a proper pirate. Yeller was never the pirate's colour."

McGoon squirmed and spluttered, but eventually gave in.

"Alright, I'll do as ye want, Maggie, but only the once."

Maggie looked Sloakum and McGoon up and down and sniffed.

"There'll be no trying to get yer hands on treasure, neither, Jonah Sloakum. Not till we've spied out what's there anyway. We'll go down all nicey-nicey. Now, while we're on that subject, the pair of ye look like ye've been dragged through a mangle. Ye can't go down there looking like that. Ye'll be eaten alive. What did ye say these monks ye saw was wearing, Dick McGoon?"

McGoon looked startled.

"Wearing? I wasn't looking out fer the way they was dressed, Maggie. They was all out to kill us."

"Yes, but you seen 'em, didn't yer?" said Maggie impatiently. "Ye must have noticed how they looked."

McGoon shrugged.

"We didn't see much of their faces. They was all dressed in hoods and long coats."

"That's it then," said Maggie. "We'll go in hoods and long coats. Have ye anything like that on this ship, Jonah Sloakum?"

Sloakum snorted.

"What'd I want with hoods and long coats?"

"Well, ye need 'em now." said Maggie. "Have ye anyone as can make 'em fer us?"

Sloakum looked around.

"Well, there's Thimblerigger Joe. He said he was a tailor before he started his cheating ways."

"Right," said Maggie. "Get him working on something useful for once in his useless life."

***

Three hooded figures descended the steps of a transporter and surveyed the scene. A reddish sun hung low in the sky. Everything in the desolate landscape – even the low, scrubby bushes – appeared to be grey.

"No wonder they're all saying their prayers here," said Maggie. "I'd be saying mine to get out pronto."

Sloakum's temper had not improved.

"I told yer Fancypants wouldn't be seen dead in a place like this. He'll be off somewhere, flaunting hisself like a Lascassian hoorie."

Maggie gave him a scornful look.

"Hush yer moaning, Jonah Sloakum. We've work to do. Let's find someone or something that might know what's happening in this pox-ridden place. What's that over there?" she asked, pointing.

In the distance they could make out a dark shape, half hidden in the mist.

"Looks like it may be a house," said McGoon.

"Right, let's start there," said Maggie.

Sloakum drew his cutlass.

"I ain't taking no chances, Maggie, after what I heard."

McGoon nodded.

"That blaster ye've got, Maggie, won't be no use neither. They'll be all over ye before ye can move."

Maggie gave another scornful look.

"A right pair of chicken-hearts ye are. Stay here, if ye have not the stomach."

Off she strode, the other two following behind her, grumbling. The building was further away and bigger than they had first thought. They trudged for more than an hour through scrub until they found themselves in front of an enormous white stone building fronted by stone columns, with spires at either end and a roof adorned with rounded turrets. Statues of figures in robes stood in niches around its walls and the front was covered in stone carvings. A stone path led up to a massive door, on one side of which dangled a rope. Maggie gave it a pull and a second or two later they heard a bell clang in the distance. They waited, but nothing appeared to be happening. Maggie gave the rope another pull and again a bell sounded. A few seconds later the door was opened by a figure dressed in a black robe. When he saw Sloakum, McGoon and Maggie, he crossed himself with his right hand and then, without speaking, gestured them to enter. He led them through a series of long galleries that became ever more richly decorated with carvings, sculptures, tapestries and paintings, until they emerged into a vast pillaried basilica. At one end they could see several rows of purple-clad figures seated before a large marble table, on which was a gold tabernacle and a number of gold vessels encrusted with precious stones. In front, sitting on a gold throne, was an elderly man, dressed in a white, full-length robe and white skullcap. Other figures strode to and fro before the table, making gestures and intoning incantations, while in a gallery, a choir and orchestra periodically struck up.

Sloakum looked around, gazing appreciatively at all the gold and jewels on display and wondering how he might get his hands on it. Maggie sniffed the aromatic air.

"What's that smell?" she whispered.

"I think it's incense," McGoon whispered back. "I took some in a prize, one time. Sold it for a good price. There's plenty as will pay well for it."

Finally the music died down and the ceremony seemed to be over. The figure that had led them gestured to them to go forward towards the man in white. He gazed at them benignly.

"Welcome, welcome. All true believers are welcome here. Pray, do tell, what order commands you?"

For several seconds there was silence. Then Sloakum spoke.

"Orders? I don't take no orders from no one. I gives orders."

The man in white continued to smile benignly.

"I see from your apparel you are creatures of sanctity. Where is your chapter house, your abode, the place from which you venture forth to preach the eternal verities?"

Again there was silence.

This time, Maggie replied.

"Are ye talking about our ship?"

The man in white nodded gravely.

"Ah, your ship, I see. You are a mendicant order. You travel the Galaxy to bring the Word to the unenlightened. What, pray, is the name of this holy ship?"

There was another silence, then Sloakum answered.

"*Rum, Sodomy and the Lash.*"

The man in white looked at them in astonishment and crossed himself, while murmurs of surprise arose from those seated.

"All glory to the Almighty. From your answer, you must be members of the Alcocatamites, our most exalted order, revered for its sanctity. You departed aeons ago to spread the word of the one true religion that worshipped the one true God. Now you have returned to us, to our immense joy."

He held up both hands in a gesture of welcome, as the others rose from their seats and applauded, letting out shouts of exultation.

"You must bring us word of your missions, of the souls that you have saved, of the devotees you have brought to our faith. You must enlighten us, so that we might strengthen our devotion."

Sloakum, McGoon and Maggie stared at him, unable to respond.

"You must tell us," he continued, "how you have told the godless multitude that the only way to paradise is to obey every word of the Almighty One."

Maggie realized she had to respond.

"Yes, we do put it about a bit. We don't stand no nonsense."

The man in white raised his hand in acknowledgement

"Praise be for your faithful adherence. I see, too, that you still practice mortification of the flesh," he said. "So refreshing in this age of indulgence."

The three looked at each other in incomprehension.

"Pardon?" said Maggie.

"You mentioned the word 'lash'. I take it that you still employ flagellation in your religious practices to dispel the insidious demons of softness, pessimism and lukewarm faith that dominate the lives of so many. What is your preferred organ of flagellation?"

"Pardon?" said Maggie again.

"What type of lash do you use?"

Sloakum gave him a gimlet-eyed look.

"The cat o' nine tails, of course."

The man in white pondered this.

"The cat o' nine tails is not mentioned in our breviary as a method of mortification. Perhaps time has erased it from our memory. Does it have the required effect? Does it remind the flagellants of the fleeting nature of their existence, deter them from concupiscence and encourage them to make true repentance?"

Sloakum had no idea, but he knew what the cat could do.

"Nothing like it fer keeping a scurvy crew on their toes. Makes 'em toe the line, 'cos they know they'll get even worse if they don't."

The man in white nodded even more gravely.

"It sounds a most condign mortification. You must enlighten me about this cat o' nine tails. I shall revive its use and encourage our postulants to employ it in their devotions. Now I must introduce myself," he said, the benign smile returning. "I am His Holiness, the Supreme Ecclesiarch Adeodatus the Six Hundred and Fifty-seventh, and these," he added, pointing to the purple-clad assembly, "are the Ordinals of the one true church, the Sempiternal Ecclesia, that sent your forebears out on their sacred mission. Will you tell me the names by which you undertake your holy mission?"

Maggie looked at him, not quite comprehending.

"You want to know our names?"

"Of course. Not the names that an ungodly world first gave you, but the names that your order bestowed upon you when it sent you forth to do your holy work."

Maggie's comprehension had not improved.

"The name's Maggie."

"Welcome Most Reverend Maggie," said the Ecclesiarch. "And who are your companions?"

Maggie now realized what he had meant.

"This is Jonah and this is Dick."

"Welcome, too, Most Reverends Jonah and Dick. We all worship the one, true God. All other gods are false gods. Heed them at your peril."

Maggie surveyed the faces of the Supreme Ecclesiarch and the Ordinals and realized that they were looking at her, Sloakum and McGoon with something approaching reverence. This was an opportunity. Sloakum and McGoon might be too dumb to see it, but she wasn't one for turning an opportunity down.

"Thankee fer yer welcome. Most kind. As ye say, we've come a long way. We're hunting a villain who's done no end of wrong and thought maybe ye could help us find him."

The Ecclesiarch's eyes narrowed.

"What is he – a heretic, a schismatic, an infidel, an unbeliever, a blasphemer, a sinner?"

Maggie nodded vigorously.

"Oh, he's all of those things, Your Worship, and much more besides. You wouldn't believe how deep-dyed a villain he is. The worst ever seen."

Adeodatus the Six Hundred and Fifty-seventh adopted his gravest expression.

"Such wrongdoing is worthy of the most severe punishment. I shall personally call down the wrath of the Almighty upon him."

"That's very kind of ye, Your Worship. He's supposed to be in these parts and we was hoping ye might be able to help us find him. Name of de la Beche. Calls hisself 'Captain' and puts on all sorts of airs. Ye'd know him if ye saw him. Dresses all fancy, like …" she looked around at the Ecclesiarch and the Ordinals, "well, fancy, as I said. He's here looking for something that don't belong to him. Very sacred it is, to some others. They was most upset to lose it and they wouldn't like de la Beche to get his paws on it, 'cos then they wouldn't never see it again and it would spoil all their worshippings something rotten."

Adeodatus the Six Hundred and Fifty-seventh clapped his hands. From out of a side door there appeared a number of men wearing chain mail and helmets and carrying large axes. They marched briskly towards the Ecclesiarch.

"These are soldiers of our Holy Guard. They ensure order among those who believe and exact retribution on those who do not. I shall issue instructions to them that this villain is to be apprehended. How would you like him punished? We have the rack, the axe or burning at the stake. Burning at the stake is usually reserved for heretics," he added, "but, since this person's actions seem to cover the gamut of misdeeds, we could make an exception for him. As it happens, the ceremony you have just witnessed is the first part of a pyrofixion. I think you would be very interested in seeing the rest of it."

He saw that they were staring at him, uncomprehending.

"Let me explain. Pyrofixion is the ceremony by which heretics are given their deserved punishment. After we, the faithful, have renewed our allegiance to the one true God, the heretics are led to the appointed place and reminded of their wrongdoing. Let us go."

Four liveried attendants appeared, carrying a chair lined with velvet and decorated with elaborate gold scrolling. They lowered it so that Adeodatus could sit, and then carried him out of the basilica, with Maggie, Sloakum and McGoon in attendance, accompanied by triumphant sounds from choir and orchestra, leading the rest of the congregation in procession.

They emerged into a large square. In the middle they could see a pillar surrounded by a raised platform, under which were piles of wood. Adeodatus gave a signal and, from one corner of the square, three figures were led towards the platform, heads bowed down. Another figure, dressed in richly-embroidered robes, stepped forward and read from a scroll. On hearing him, two of the condemned uttered shouts and fell to their knees, kissing the ground.

"They have been spared death," said Adeodatus. "They will only have to spend twenty years in a penitential priory, where they will be scourged daily."

The two were led away. The third was taken up steps to the platform and tied to the pillar. The wood underneath was lit and the flames began to lick upwards. The condemned began to scream and writhe as the flames reached him and his robes caught alight. Suddenly there was a loud bang; the entire scene was hidden in a cloud of smoke. As it cleared, they could see the remains of a torso still tied to the stake, while all around the now-shattered platform were parts of a body.

"We have been merciful," said Adeodatus. "Blasting powder was tied to his body and, as the flames did their work, it exploded. He did not have to endure too long."

Sloakum had been watching events with mounting appreciation.

"I think I've been too soft with stringin' up, Maggie. I'll have to try a bit of that next time," he said, in a low voice.

"Ye couldn't do it on yer ship, Jonah Sloakum," Maggie answered in a withering whisper.

"No, it would have to wait till we got ashore, but it's given me a few ideas."

Adeodatus finished receiving obeisance from members of the congregation and turned to them.

"Is that the punishment this villain should receive?"

Maggie gave Sloakum a dig in the ribs, fearful that he would agree. He got the message.

"Very kind of ye, Your Worship. If it was up to me I'd have him strung up before Davy Jones could shake a manacle, but we've been asked special by the ones he's stealing from to take him alive. They're very God-fearing sorts, ye see, and they've got their very own types of punishment fer the likes of him."

The Ecclesiarch nodded.

"Most becoming sentiments. My instruction will be that he is taken alive. Now I expect you will want to ensure success by undergoing a course of prayer and abstinence. I shall appoint a most rigorous chaplain for you, who will oversee all your devotions. If you have your cat o' nine tails with you, I'm sure he can be persuaded to administer it. Mortification of the flesh is the surest way of achieving the object of prayer."

Sloakum looked thunderstruck. McGoon's mouth opened and closed with a gurgling sound. Maggie managed to speak.

"It might be a bit soon for that, Yer Worship. Maybe we could do that after we've caught him?"

The Ecclesiarch pondered this.

"Perhaps you are right. We sometimes presume on the wishes and inclinations of the Almighty. He can act in mysterious ways, you know. We shall join you in your quest and when, by the grace of the Almighty, we succeed, we shall worship Him together."

3

The road ahead led into a forest of small trees. Jim shaded his eyes and squinted. The sun, although not bright, was low, shining directly into his face.

"Anywhere else," said de la Beche, as they waited where Bon August had told them, "I would have said that a road would be bound to lead somewhere, but in this place I would not be so sure."

He was dressed, as he said, for "the country", in matching three-quarter-length check tweed skirt and cloak, *eau de nil* ruched blouse, fastened with a large amethyst brooch, long leather boots and a wide-brimmed hat.

"I rather agree Sechy." Said Doctor Culpepper as the three of them scanned the road. Just then, Jim heard an odd sound – regular, sharp clicks. Out of the forest appeared what at first sight he thought were apparitions – creatures of a sort he had never seen before. They walked on four legs; on their backs were large protuberances that glinted in the sunlight. As they got nearer he saw that the protuberances were figures, clad from head to toe in what looked like metal, riding along the road on brownish-grey, four-legged animals. They approached until they were very close, then stopped. One figure raised a visor, revealing a bearded, weather-beaten face, and then spoke in a deep voice.

"Soothly, I dare well say that I have ne'er seen that which more resembled villeins and vagabonds than that which is before me. Make answer whence ye came, for I wist well that ye are not of this world."

Jim stared at him, bemused.

"Not quite sure I caught that, darling," said de la Beche. "Perhaps you might care to repeat it."

The metallic figure glowered at him and then gave a roar and drew out a sword.

"It beseemeth me that ye betoken the duress of the world and the great sin against all that is holy. For that I shall smite thee and cleave thee in twain."

"I think I catch your drift now," said de la Beche, stepping back hurriedly. "No need for fisticuffs. I am sure we can discuss things amicably."

Just then, Jim noticed another figure, little more than a youth, on foot and wearing a leather singlet and trousers. come forward.

"Perhaps I can help, Squire. You really don't want to get on the wrong side of Sir Agravain. He's a bit touchy this morning."

De la Beche looked him up and down.

"I have no wish to get on the wrong side of anybody, darling. What makes him talk like that?"

"He talks Knightly, Squire. That's because he's a Knight of the Sacred Circle. They all talk like that." He turned towards the Knight. "Hold, good Sir Agravain, I fain would parlay."

The Knight grunted and resheathed his sword.

"I see you can talk this Knightly, too," said de la Beche, sounding surprised. "Who are you?"

"I'm a squire, Squire," came the reply.

"A 'squire squire'?"

"No, just a squire. I call you Squire – a bit of respect – but I *am* a squire. So we're all squire, if you see what I mean."

De la Beche shrugged.

"Not sure I do, darling, but never mind. What does a squire do?"

"I'm like an agent. I look after all the contracts, keep the books, make sure they know what they're supposed to be doing – all that sort of thing."

De la Beche could not repress a laugh.

"I confess I'm not very well up on what Knights do, but I thought they were free spirits, roaming the country performing brave deeds in the name of – what is it called – chivalry?"

The squire gave a contemptuous snort.

"Who told you that! Honestly, people have no idea of what it costs to be a Knight. They've got overheads: castles to run, fiery steeds to keep, tournaments to organize – to say nothing of the feasts. None of that comes cheap, you know."

De la Beche managed a sympathetic nod.

"I had no idea, darling. Thank you for enlightening me. Castles I can understand would be expensive. Fiery steeds? What are they?"

"You're looking at them," said the Squire, in surprised tones.

Jim looked. All he saw were rather bedraggled quadrupeds, with large square heads and pointed ears, sagging under the weight of armoured riders almost as big as they were.

"If you don't mind me saying so," said de la Beche, "they're not very big."

The Squire looked affronted.

"I didn't say they were big. I said they were fiery."

"Fiery is as fiery does, I suppose," said de la Beche. "I think they're rather sweet. What's this one called?" he said, pointing to Sir Agravain's mount.

"Daisy."

"Daisy. Fascinating. From where I am standing, it appears to be of the male gender, but Daisy is normally …"

"I know, I know," said the Squire. "A girl's name. But Daisy is – how can I put it?" He made a rocking motion with his hand.

"Confused?"

"Exactly, Squire: confused."

"Fiery and confused, a fearsome combination. Do tell, what sort of animal is Daisy?"

The Squire hesitated, pursing his lips.

"Technically, it's called a donkey."

"Technically?"

"Well, yes, it actually is called a donkey."

"And for what purpose does a Knight need a donkey?" asked de la Beche.

Again, the Squire seemed affronted.

"A Knight needs a fiery steed for everything he does – rescuing damsels in distress, slaying dragons and the rest."

"Most interesting," said de la Beche. "Are there dragons here?"

"Could be," said the Squire, rather defensively, Jim thought

"And have any of these brave Knights actually slain one?"

"Not yet," came the answer, in an even more defensive tone.

"What about damsels in distress? I understood that females weren't allowed on this planet."

"Technically speaking, you're right, but, if they were, they could rescue them."

"Most gallant of them, I'm sure. Is there anything else they do?"

The Squire shrugged and sighed.

"What do you think? They uphold righteousness and right wrongs wherever they find them. Then there are Grail quests, but, to tell the truth, we haven't had one of them for ages. Grail quests seem to have gone out of fashion these days."

Jim saw a smile appear on de la Beche's face.

"Ah, now that is something we might be able to discuss, darling. Allow me to introduce myself. I am Sir Sechaverell de la Beche, *bart*, captain of HMS *Bountiful*. These are my companions, Doctor Cuthbert Culpepper, the ship's doctor, and Jim, the cabin boy. To whom do I have the pleasure of talking?"

"Squire."

"I know what you do, darling. What are you called?"

"Squire Squire. Squire's my name, squire's what I do. I like to keep things simple. What did you say your name was?"

"Sir Sechaverall de la Beche."

"*Sir* Sechaverall. Does that mean you're a Knight, too?"

"Strictly speaking, I am a baronet, which is a notch above a Knight, but let's not quibble about titles. Now, let me put you in the picture. We have been charged with recovering an object sacred to the denizens of a certain planet that we have reason to believe is somewhere here. That, I understand, corresponds with the definition of a Grail and these brave Knights, I am told, are Grail-finders nonpareil."

Squire Squire began to look interested.

"Maybe we could do business. What is this object?"

"It's called the Holly Kwokkah."

"Funny name for a Grail. What does it look like?"

"We're not sure. It could be a cup, or a bowl of some sort."

"Any idea where it might be or who has it?"

"Not at the moment. Its whereabouts are a complete mystery."

Squire Squire shook his head and looked very sceptical.

"You don't know what it looks like and you don't know where it is. This is going to cost you."

De la Beche nodded.

"We understand, of course, that there will be a fee and we are willing to pay for the right result."

Squire Squire shook his head again.

"There are no guarantees in the Grail business. The Knights of the Sacred Circle are Grail-Questers, not Grail-Finders. Frankly, from what you've said, this Kwokkah might not even exist. If we gave you a guarantee, we could spend all our time looking for it and not finding it, and then where would we be? Out of business, that's where. Our contract is on a strictly *per diem* basis. Take it or leave it."

It was de la Beche's turn to look sceptical.

"Come now, darling. This whole planet is about giving guarantees. Do the right thing and you get the keys to Paradise. Isn't that the message that they all sell here?"

Squire Squire shrugged.

"They can say what they like. No one has ever come back from Paradise saying it isn't all it's cracked up to be and wanting their money back. Guarantees like that I could give any day, but not for Grails. They don't find easy."

De la Beche paused and looked at his companions, then turned back to Squire Squire.

"I always find haggling a little unseemly. Tell me your rate."

"What money are you paying in?"

"The best: Galactos."

Squire Squire thought for a few moments.

"In that case, I can give you a discount on our normal Grail rates. Call it two hundred a day, plus fifty a day steed supplement."

De la Beche rolled his eyes.

"That is very steep – and do you really need donkeys for this sort of work?"

Squire Squire was unmoved.

"Nobody takes Knights seriously if they are not mounted on their fiery steeds. As I said, take it or leave it."

"How long do you think it might take?"

Squire Squire spread his arms and shrugged.

"How can I say? Might take a day, might take a year. I did hear of one Grail quest that lasted a century – though, if it went on that long, we would give you a bigger discount."

"Very considerate of you, darling. Let's try it for ten days and see how we get on."

Squire Squire nodded and turned to the Knights.

"All hail, Sir Agravain and Knights of the Sacred Circle. As the order of true chivalry demandeth, ye shall go forth and help seek a Holy Grail at a rate of two hundred Galactos per day, plus fifty Galactos steed supplement. Beseemeth ye that is meet and good?"

A chorus of assent arose from the Knights. Squire Squire extended his hand.

"You've got a deal, Squire, and when the Knights of the Sacred Circle do a deal they always celebrate with a feast in their castle. I hope you'll join us."

"Delighted, I'm sure. Where is this castle?"

Squire Squire pointed towards the forest. "It's a few hours from here."

As they set out, de la Beche surveyed the retinue of Knights.

"Tell me, darling," he said to Squire Squire, "where do these Knights come from and what is this Sacred Circle?"

"Long story," came the reply.

"I think we have a bit of time."

Squire Squire paused before answering.

"Well, there was this king ..."

4

The Lord High Admiral of the Orsonian Battle Fleet gazed in the mirror, and felt a twinge of concern. Were the lines on his face a little deeper and more numerous? Was the flesh around cheek and jaw beginning to sag? Was there just a trace of dewlap on the neck? And did there seem to be more hairs left on the comb that morning? He turned his face to show more of his best profile, shifted in his seat to get a more favourable light and decided that there was no need to worry. Just to be sure, he would consult a cosmetic surgeon. A little tightening here and there might allow him to cut an even finer figure before the Orsonian public and make him even more attractive to wives and mistresses. They did pay attention to these things.

It was not as if he didn't have plenty of other things to worry about. He had become aware that there were mutterings of discontent everywhere. The Nullarborean situation was getting worse rapidly. The Arcturan debacle had become common knowledge and had led to a lot of unwelcome comments, not just about the appallingly high price of Chelodoney in the shops. The armchair militarists on the Ruling Council called him weak and vacillating. The Arcturans had been there for the taking. He should have acted alone, without the notoriously perfidious Southern Cross. The lily-livered bureaucrats on the Council, on the other hand, claimed to be appalled at how he could be so cavalier with the peace of the Galaxy. There were mutterings, too, about his high-handedness and vanity and whether he was getting a bit long in the tooth. He had heard that some of his underlings in the Fleet were secretly jockeying for position in the expectation that he would soon retire or, failing that, be culled.

The collection of gold had stalled. He had no idea if there were enough doubloons, or whatever they were called, to pay off Sloa-kum, if he ever found de la Beche. On top of everything, his wives and mistresses had become more demanding than ever. If it wasn't about gold – or the lack of it – it was about their allow-ances and, though he could scarcely credit it, about the attention he paid to them and his performance. He had been tired on occa-sions. Who wouldn't be, after all he had to put up with? Given the style in which he kept them, what had they to complain about?

***

Civil Servant 21346 gazed with a mixture of glee and envy at the latest edition of the *Galactic Inquirer* as it appeared on his screen. It had taken its revelations about the Lord High Admiral to a whole new level. All four of his wives, it seemed, were flaunt-ing themselves with his rivals in Orsonian high society, while an enterprising agent was purporting to have several of the Admiral's mistresses on offer to the highest bidder. For one fleeting moment he thought he might bid, but then discovered that the price was more than he could ever afford. Then something else in the *In-quirer* caught his eye.

Manifesto of the Populist Party

Preamble

A spectre is haunting Orson – the spectre of populism. The history of Orson has hitherto been the history of one class appropriating to itself the fruits of an entire empire. It has instilled in all subject populations the false notion that, as the heirs and descendants of those who established the empire, only they can maintain civilized order. They do so with the aid of a collusive religious hierarchy, who share many of their privileges. Between them they claim to be the pillars upon which Orsonian civilization rests, and so justify the oppression of all other elements of society. In reality, the ruling class and their religious collaborators are utterly parasitic. They produce nothing and consume everything. Until now, the rest of the population – those who produce the wealth – have accepted this state of affairs, duped by notions that they shared in the glories of empire. Now, those delusions are being exposed everywhere. The Orsonian people are beginning to realize that the ruling class has become ever more flagrant and arrogant in its abuse of power. Resistance is growing. At present, the resistance must remain clandestine, but the tide is irresistible. Nothing can hold it back. Soon it will sweep away all remnants of the old order.

Freedom is our destiny.

Power to the people.

The hairs on the neck of Civil Servant 21346 stood up and he felt a distinct tumescence. This manifesto had put into words what he had long felt. He needed to find out more. There was a link on the passage. He followed it and saw a single word:

Organize

He stared at it, wondering what he should do, when it faded and more words appeared:

Begin, and we will contact you.

His heart was racing and he was breathing heavily. How to begin? He would make some tentative enquiries on the underground network. Then another thought occurred. Perhaps this was a trick. Perhaps the Orsonian powers had inserted this passage into the *Inquirer* to flush out would-be traitors. He doubted that the Admiral had the imagination for such a ruse, especially as he loathed the *Inquirer*, but there were others who might well have done it. He would have to proceed very carefully. Then he heard an all too familiar voice.

"Civil Servant 21346, come in here."

He entered the Admiral's office to find him affecting his usual officious expression, but Civil Servant 21346 thought he detected a trace of anxiety behind it.

"Civil Servant 21346, have you been in contact with Captain Sloakum recently?"

That was an easy one to stonewall. Civil Servant 21346 liked easy ones.

"We believe Captain Sloakum is on Utrophia, Lord High Admiral."

"I know that," said the Admiral, unable to keep a trace of exasperation out of his voice. "Have you been in contact with him?"

Another easy one.

"Under Legex Code 2314, only the recognized religious authorities are permitted to communicate with Utrophia, Lord High Admiral."

A detailed knowledge of the Orsonian legal system was not the Admiral's forte. Bluster and bullying were.

"Yes, yes. I meant, of course, have you contacted the religious authorities to see if they have been in contact with him?"

This was becoming too easy. Civil Servant 21346 hardly had to think.

"Under Legex Code 4715, Lord High Admiral, members of the Civil Service are forbidden from requesting information from the religious authorities that is not of a religious or ceremonial nature. Such a request can only come from an appointed authority, such as yourself."

The Admiral gave Civil Servant 21346 his most baleful stare. The fact that this upstart functionary was almost certainly correct made him even more annoyed. His exasperation was further increased when he realized that he would have to make the request to the High Priest, who combined a strict and unbending stance on all questions of religion with an utterly uncooperative attitude to everything else. He had no choice. He needed to know whether Sloakum had caught de la Beche, so he could hand that double-dealing dandy over to the Nullarboreans. He would tell them that de la Beche was the villain who had stolen the Kwok-kah, despite the best efforts of the Orsonians to return it to their rightful owners. In their gratitude, they would defect to the Orsonians, leaving a gaping hole in the Southern Cross Federation defences and consolidating the Admiral's reputation as the great defender of the Orsonian Empire. Questioning his position would then be treason.

He resigned himself to making the request.

"Contact the High Priest. Ask him if he would be so good as to come to see me."

Civil Servant 21346 made the call. The High Priest's secretary was dismissive. "His Exalted Sanctity has many engagements. I do not see any gaps in his diary at present."

Civil Servant 21346 pressed the point. The Lord High Admiral was most anxious for a discussion. The secretary said sniffily that he would mention it to the High Priest, but could not confirm anything.

A day later, the High Priest arrived. The Admiral attempted to greet him convivially, something for which he had absolutely no talent, but the High Priest was his usual brusque self, rejecting the refreshments offered.

"Why do you want to see me?"

The Admiral smiled his most unctuous smile.

"I thought it would be a good idea, Your Exalted Sanctity, if we lords spiritual and temporal meet from time to time to exchange views and to discuss how we might improve the moral health of the Empire."

The High Priest looked at the Admiral as if he thought he had gone slightly mad.

"This idea has just occurred to you, has it?"

"No, of course not, but, as I'm sure you realize, I have been very busy of late. Nevertheless I am determined to make time for what I think is a most important idea."

The High Priest looked less than impressed.

"And I'm sure you realize that I never stop preaching about the moral health of the Empire and I have yet to see improvement. I don't think our little chat will make much difference. Now, what is it you really wanted to talk to me about?"

For a few seconds, the Admiral was disconcerted, then the unctuous smile returned.

"The other thing that I thought I might mention, Your Exalted Sanctity, was whether you had been in communication with Utrophia lately?"

The expression on the High Priest's face suggested he thought the Admiral was definitely going mad.

"Why would I do that?"

"I thought you, as the senior religious figure in the Empire, would be in regular communication with your fellows on Utrophia."

"Not at all. Besides, our 'fellows' on Utrophia, as you call them, are members of the Order of Ambelica."

The Admiral was puzzled.

"Forgive me. What does the Order of Ambelica have to do with it?"

"They have taken a vow of silence."

The Admiral could not quite believe what he had heard.

"What do you mean, a vow of silence?"

The High Priest's suspicions of the Admiral's sanity were rapidly being confirmed.

"I would have thought that was obvious."

The Admiral's disbelief was now total.

"Are you saying that you could not communicate with Utrophia even if you wanted to?"

The High Priest agreed.

"Of course not. Utrophia is best left to itself, to do what it does best. That is why we sent the Ambelicans. Their prayers and invocations are what is needed to improve the moral health of the Empire. They are not distracted from praying by idle chatter."

The Admiral watched as the High Priest gave a ritual blessing and left. He felt a grey mist enveloping his brain. He had always thought of himself as a believer, but realized that he would never truly understand the religious mind. More importantly, the religious mind was not going to help him find Sloakum.

***

Civil Servant 21346 began to fantasize about being a leader of the forthcoming revolution. He was, of course, ideally placed to take over the Admiral's role in external relations with the rest of the Galaxy. He would, naturally, be allowed to enjoy possession of the by then former Admiral's palace and estates. Some restraint would be necessary. The revolutionaries could not simply ape the manners and actions of the old ruling class. He would take only two – or at most four – of the Admiral's mistresses and would relegate one of his wives to concubine and make her a housemaid.

He scrutinized the messages coming over the underground network. They always had a rebellious air to them, but until now it had been little more than powerless underlings airing their frustration. He looked for signs that things might be changing. He thought he detected that frustration was increasing and turning, perhaps, to anger, but was he reading too much into a few gripes? What was it that the *Manifesto* urged? *Organize.* Was the time right to break cover? What was it the *Manifesto* also said? *Begin, and we will contact you.* How to begin? He sat, pondering, in an agony of indecision.

5

They trudged through the forest for about an hour. The trees rose straight and high from the side of the road. Jim peered in, but could see little in the gloom. Only an occasional sound, part roar, part wail, that he thought might have been an animal, pierced the silence. Eventually, they emerged into a wide plain. In the distance, he could see several plumes of smoke. He asked what was burning.

"It's probably a battle," replied Squire Squire. "There's usually one going on somewhere."

Jim was taken aback.

"A battle? Who is doing the fighting?"

"Could be any of them. They're always at each others' throats."

"Are you saying the religions fight amongst themselves?" asked de la Beche.

Squire Squire looked at him, surprised.

"Too right, they do."

They drew near to one of the smoke plumes. Jim saw it came from a burning building. Squire Squire motioned the party to halt, and he and one of the Knights went to inspect the still-smouldering remains.

"Looks like it was one of the Silurian abbeys," he said on returning. "There are a few bodies in there, but everything's too burnt, so I can't really tell."

"I see what you mean about being at each others' throats," said de la Beche. "Who do you think did it?"

"I expect it was the Ordovicians. They don't like the Silurians because the Silurians believe in the God of Love."

"How quaint of them. And what do the Ordovicians believe?"

"They believe in the God of Peace."

"Yes, I quite see how they couldn't stand each other."

They went on and came to another burning building. Squire Squire again examined it.

"This one's definitely Ordovician. Some of their symbols are still on the walls. It looks like the Silurians gave as good as they got."

"Were there any bodies?" asked Jim.

"Only a couple. You couldn't really call it a battle. Just a little skirmish."

They went on for another hour, passing several more ruins, remnants of past battles, but saw no signs of life except a few large, black birds that croaked loudly as they went by. The road began to rise from the plain , winding through a series of low hills. As they rounded a bend, Jim stopped abruptly, shocked to the core. He found himself looking at a wooden gibbet, from which hung four bodies, swinging slowly in the wind. In front of the gibbet a large sign read:

> The villains must be hung, sliced, stabbed, secretly and
> publicly, by those who can, like one must kill a rabid dog

"More from the Gods of Love and Peace, I take it?" said de la Beche.

"No, it was just a peasants' revolt," replied Squire Squire.

"A what?"

"Religious bigwigs don't like getting their hands dirty. They have peasants to do stuff like washing and cleaning and growing food. Sometimes the peasants get uppity and revolt, so their masters think they need to be taught a lesson to keep the others in line. That's holy types for you."

Jim stared in horrified fascination at the bodies, unable to speak.

"I take it that you would not describe yourself as a 'holy type', darling," said de la Beche, "but what about your Knights of the Sacred Circle? I assume they are holy types, but from what I see, they are not above waving their swords with intent."

Squire Squire nodded in acknowledgement.

"That's true, but they're Knights. 'Slay and pray' is their motto. That's what Knights do. You know where you are with Knights."

They reached the crest of a hill and, looking down, Jim caught sight of the castle. It reminded him of a sight he had once seen as a child, a large stone building, rising high out of a flat plain, topped with turrets and battlements and surrounded by a moat. They were walking a little behind the Knights to avoid the smell of the donkeys.

"Tell me," de la Beche asked Squire Squire, "You strike me as a very smart young man. What brought you here?"

Squire Squire grimaced.

"Another long story. Put it down to damsels."

"But there are no damsels here."

"Not here. Back on my home planet."

"Don't tell me you rescued damsels in distress there."

Squire Squire grimaced again.

"Not exactly. I got them into distress, if you know what I mean. Their fathers didn't take too kindly to me, so I had to make myself scarce. They'll never find me here."

They walked towards the castle and onto a wooden bridge that hung from chains over the moat. As they entered, Jim glanced up and saw a large metal grille hanging down from the castle wall.

"That's the portcullis," said Squire Squire. "We put it down at night after we lift the drawbridge. It keeps marauders out."

"Do you have marauders?" asked Doctor Culpepper, sounding surprised.

"You bet," said Squire Squire. "You wouldn't believe what some of these holy types get up to. They would take anything not nailed down, and slit your throat as soon as look at you, all the time thanking their gods for being such good boys."

They entered a large courtyard. The Knights dismounted and were helped out of their armour by retainers, while others led the donkeys off. Squire Squire motioned de la Beche and his party to follow him. They went through a high wooden door and then through a number of rooms hung with tapestries depicting knights in scenes of chivalric valour. Eventually they reached a large hall with a high vaulted ceiling, its walls decorated with heraldic shields and assorted weaponry. In the middle, was a massive, round table with painted segments depicting all sorts of animals and plants. Around it were high-backed carved chairs. Squire Squire pointed to a bench and told them to sit there to await the Knights.

As they waited, more retainers came in, carrying food and drink for the feasts. Jim watched as salvers of meat and fish and bird, bowls of fruit, loaves of bread, platters of vegetables, and flagons of wine were arranged on the table. A small table was set down near them and more food and drink was placed on it. He heard a noise at the other end of the hall, and saw several figures carrying musical instruments. One began to blow a bugle and through a door in the middle of the hall, the Knights entered in procession and sat down around the table, occupying all the chairs but one.

Squire Squire indicated that they should sit at the nearby table. As they sat down, Sir Agravain rose and in a loud voice said, "Gentil knight, Sir Sechaverell, wilt thou not join us at the Circle Sacred for our feast?"

"Certainly, darling," replied de la Beche. "Only too pleased."

He walked over to the table and sat in the empty chair. As he did so, the Knights stopped eating and turned to stare at him. Jim glanced at Squire Squire and saw a look of alarm on his face. He asked him what was wrong.

"That's the Siege Perilous," came the reply.

"The what?" said Jim.

"The Siege Perilous. It is said that only the Chosen One can sit in that seat and live. No one has dared to sit in it for over a hundred years."

Jim looked over to the table and saw de la Beche tucking in to the food and drink with apparent gusto. One by one, the Knights raised a glass to de la Beche and then began to eat too.

"He's not dead yet. Who is this Chosen One?" said Jim.

Squire Squire shook his head.

"Who knows? I have only been told that a Knight who sits in the Siege Perilous and lives will do great deeds."

"What great deeds?"

Squire Squire gave an exasperated sigh.

"Knightly stuff: adventures, slaying dragons, all that kind of thing."

"So, if the Captain can sit in the Siege Perilous and live, is he the Chosen One?"

Squire Squire shrugged.

"Maybe. Who knows?"

Jim had his doubts. He turned to Doctor Culpepper. Did he think de la Beche was about to do great knightly deeds?

"Frankly, dear boy, I don't think Sechy would be seen dead on a donkey," said Doctor Culpepper. "It's not really his thing, is it? Besides, I'm sure he would say that he doesn't have a thing to wear for riding."

They turned to look at the table and saw all the Knights in boisterous mood, exchanging toasts with de la Beche and each other.

"Chosen or not," said Squire Squire, "one who sits in the Siege Perilous and lives is a Knight of the Sacred Circle."

"Will that help in the search for the Grail – I mean the Kwokkah?" asked Jim.

"May do," said Squire Squire. "You can never tell. Grail quests can be tricky."

Jim had to agree about the trickiness of Grail quests. Maybe that wasn't the only thing that was tricky.

"There are a lot of religions on this planet. Which one do the Knights believe in?"

Squire Squire looked surprised.

"All of them, of course."

It was Jim's turn to be surprised.

"How can they believe in all of them? You said yourself that all these religions were at each others' throats."

Squire Squire gave him a withering look.

"That's the point. Knights uphold righteousness and right wrongs. So if one lot thinks they have been done wrong by another and asks us to put things right, for a fee, of course, we take up the banner of their God and right the wrong."

Jim was incredulous.

"So they believe in that God while they are doing it."

"Of course. They have to believe, otherwise they won't get results. That's chivalry. Anyone will tell you that."

Jim considered this, but could not see a way back into the argument. Then another thought occurred to him.

"What about the High Consistory? Where does it sit?"

The squire looked at him, uncomprehending.

"The what?"

"The High Consistory. Under the Treaty of Opiuchus, representatives of all the religions of the Galaxy are supposed to get together on Utrophia and agree on any disputes or questions put to them."

Squire Squire gave a loud guffaw.

"Religions agree? Now I've heard everything. The whole point of a religion is to disagree with every other religion. They all pretend their god loves everyone, but have you read any of their holy books? Most of them are stories of one bloodbath after another, with their gods in the thick of things. By the time you get to the end, there's practically no one left to do the worshipping. None of them can stand any of the others, so they all have their own armies. It's dog eat dog out there, believe me."

Jim found himself not entirely surprised.

"So, if they are all at each others' throats, are any of them winning?"

Squire Squire nodded.

"There are a few biggies, who like to throw their weight about. All the others just keep their heads down and chant their mumbo jumbo."

Jim was intrigued.

"Who are the biggies?"

"Well," said Squire Squire, "there is the Sempiternal Ecclesia. Nasty bunch. I'm told they come from the most miserable inhabited planet in the Galaxy, which explains a lot. They're big on torture – thumbscrews, the rack, burning oil, all that stuff. You don't want to get on the wrong side of them. Then there are the Qwezellarans. They can be just as nasty, but in a different way. They do a lot of singing and dancing and it's all lovey-dovey, but they can be fickle. If they turn nasty, then woe betide you. And then there are the Pantagnosts. I think they're a hoot. They're polytheists. They've more gods than they know what to do with. Actually you couldn't really call them gods as such. They're more like spoiled brats. They get up to things nobody else would ever dream of doing. The other religions don't know what to make of them, so they leave them alone."

Another question occurred to Jim.

"Have you ever heard of Roy Pesshe?"

Squire Squire looked startled.

"How do you know about Roy Pesshe?"

"I only know the name," Jim said "What is he – or is he an it?"

"Well," said Squire Squire, pausing between each word, "it's all about Grail quests. According to legend, to find your Grail you first have to find your Roy Pesshe."

"So how do you find your Roy Pesshe?"

"That's tricky, too."

Jim began to suspect he was hiding something.

"Have your Knights ever found a Grail?"

He had to wait for the reply.

"Not exactly."

"You mean no?"

Squire Squire pulled a face.

"You could put it like that."

"What about Roy Pesshe? Have they ever found him, or it?"

Squire Squire pulled another face.

"Not as such, no."

Jim felt the stirrings of annoyance on behalf of de la Beche.

"So you are taking money under false pretences. You know you will never be able to help us find the Kwokkah."

Squire Squire bridled at the accusation.

"Of course not. We take our Grail quests very seriously, but I did say no guarantees. Besides, now Sir Sechaverell is a Knight of the Sacred Circle, he can call on us any time he gets into trouble and we will help him out. That's worth a lot round here."

Jim thought he might have a point. Squire Squire seemed to be well informed about what was happening on Utrophia. He decided to ask him about something else.

"Do you know anything about the Bonhumes?"

Squire Squire nodded.

"Yes. Bunch of scribblers. Harmless. Nobody takes much notice of them."

"What about something called the Inquisition?"

Squire Squire made a wry face.

"What about it?"
"What is it?"
"Who knows?"
"Does it exist?"
"Who knows?"

6

Adeodatus the Six Hundred and Fifty-seventh Supreme Ecclesiarch of the Sempiternal Ecclesia, adopted his most serene expression as he looked upon the idolatrous face of the Great Sandjanum, patriarch on Utrophia of the cult of the Qwezellaran god, Qudai. The Great Sandjanum, patriarch on Utropia of Qudaism, the religion of all true Qwezallarans, likewise looked with a serene expression at the infidel Adeodatus.

They were in the Great Hall of the High Consistory, used for all meetings of religious elders on Utrophia and intended originally as the place where religious disputes could be settled harmoniously. Its elegant classical proportions and restrained décor, intended to encourage harmony, instead induced reactions from all who entered ranging from derision to nausea.

"The blessings of the one true God on you and all your followers," said Adeodatus.

"All blessings of the Supreme Qudai on you and all your followers," replied the Great Sandjanum.

"May the one true God lead you to seek peace and harmony," said Adeodatus.

"May the Supreme Qudai allow you to open your heart to truth," replied the Great Sandjanum.

"May the one true God ensure that prosperity rains upon you," said Adeodatus.

"May the Supreme Qudai ensure that you want for nothing," replied the Great Sandjanum.

They nodded to each other. The opening ritual had been satisfactorily meaningless. It was time to get down to business.

Adeodatus played his opening gambit.

"Great joy was felt in the hearts of the Supreme Ecclesia at the return of members of one of our orders, long considered lost, who had wandered the Galaxy, spreading the word of the one true God."

The Great Sandjanum felt a jolt of surprise. He regarded missionaries as the vermin of the Galaxy. The standard response to visiting missionaries on Qwezellar, as on many other planets, was summary execution. These missionaries must have been a wily bunch to have survived. He decided to remain non-committal.

"I share your joy and am humbled by your desire to share your good news with us."

Adeodatus dangled another morsel.

"Their selfless dedication has caused them to perform many great deeds on their travels. They have informed us that they are currently in pursuit of a villain that they describe as the worst sort of heretic, infidel and idolator. They intend to return him to those he has grievously wronged, for punishment."

The Great Sandjanum was puzzled. Why fuss about a single heretic, infidel and idolator? The Galaxy was stuffed full of them. What difference would one fewer make? He gave a stock response.

"May the wrath of Qudai be upon his head and may he perish at the hands of the righteous."

Adeodatus smiled inwardly. It was clear that the Great Sandjanum had no idea what he was talking about. Time to press home his advantage and enlighten him a little.

"This order, on its sacred mission to spread enlightenment and peace, has visited many worlds and has sometimes become involved in activities that can taint all who come into contact with the infidel."

The Great Sandjanum found his interest piqued. "Contact with the infidel" always meant loot of some sort.

"May you, in your wisdom, administer the penance that ensures contrition for grievous failings."

Adeodatus smiled inwardly again. The bait was being taken.

"The one true God never denies justice to those who deserve it. For contrition they must render that which they will acquire by failing to follow His law and then retire to prayer and contemplation."

The Great Sandjanum was now all ears. Locking up their own missionaries was stern stuff. Clearly, a lot of loot was involved. Was Adeodatus hinting that some might be shared?

"A judgement so wise and merciful brings blessings upon all."

Adeodatus nodded. The bait had been well and truly swallowed.

"His bounty, as His mercy, is boundless. What will be acquired is that which glitters in the eyes of all infidels and excites their lust. It must be taken from them and given to those who know it for what it should be – a means by which we can lift our eyes from this mortal sphere and contemplate the divine."

The Great Sandjanum found himself contemplating the nearest thing to the divine. No amount of gold – in vestments, in sacred vessels, in gilding, in tapestries, in frescoes and paintings – was too much for the worship of the Supreme Qudai. No prospect of more could be ignored.

"May the Supreme Qudai visit His divine punishment on all infidels who lust after its glitter and allow it to be wrought only by those dedicated to His greater glory."

Adeodatus knew he had the deal. It was only a question of settling the details.

"The name of the heretic, infidel and idolator is de la Beche. He affects the rank of Captain. He may be accompanied by familiars, whom you can dispose of as you wish. De la Beche is to be delivered to us unharmed. On delivery you will be paid an amount of gold that we will agree."

The Great Sandjanum's eyes narrowed as he stared across the table at Adeodatus, He would need a lot more information before he signed anything.

"I need to know a lot more than that before I sign anything. For a start, how much will we be paid and who is paying? Then, where is this de la Beche and who is guarding him? Finally, why do you want us to pick him up? Can't you do it yourself? Qudai knows, you have enough armed mercenaries at your disposal."

Adeodatus felt a flicker of anger, but decided that discretion was preferable.

"Our armed adherents are devoted to their sacred duties. I'm sure we both agree that a certain degree of enforcement is necessary to encourage the faithful to follow the righteous path. We have learned that de la Beche is currently enjoying the hospitality of the Knights of the Sacred Circle, with whom, as I expect you know, we do not enjoy cordial relations. We could not go and simply pluck him from their midst. We need a third party to offer him an enticement to visit."

"And how do you suggest we entice him?" said the Great Sandjanum, raising a sceptical eyebrow.

"I think there is a way. You see, de la Beche is on Utrophia seeking the Kwokkah."

"The what?"

"The Kwokkah. Apparently, it is a vessel sacred to a sect called the Nullarboreans."

"Never heard of them."

"Neither had I. I had to ask one our most learned Ordinals to find out who they were."

The Great Sandjanum shook his head, baffled.

"Kwokkahs? Nullarboreans? Where did you get all this?"

"From the Bonhumes."

The Great Sandjanum was even more baffled.

"Those petty scribblers. What do they know?"

"De la Beche visited them when he first arrived. He mentioned the Kwokkah to them."

"And they just happened to mention this to you?"

"If you drop a hint or two about the Inquisition, they will tell you everything."

The Great Sandjanum pursed his lips, sat back in his chair and considered things.

"So what are you suggesting we do?"

"You should invite de la Beche to visit you at the Grand Kalaba by telling him that you have news of the Kwokkah. Once he is there, you detain him and hand him over to us."

The Great Sandjanum considered things further. The plan had the merit of simplicity. He liked simple things.

"It sounds simple enough. I bring you back to my original question. Who pays, and how much?"

Adeodatus hesitated, trying to think of the best way to frame his answer.

"The Orsonians will be paying. I think we both agree," he continued, seeing the look of disbelief on the face of the Great Sandjanum, "that for a combination of arrogance, stupidity and avarice the Orsonians are unmatched in the Galaxy. However, I have good reason to believe that they will pay up."

"Really?" said the Great Sandjanum, still disbelieving. "What makes you think so?"

Adeodatus hesitated again.

"We have been secretly listening to the private conversations of members of our long lost order. They are most indiscreet in private and express themselves in, shall we say, an unorthodox fashion. However, it is quite clear from what they have been saying, that they have some sort of hold over the leader of the Orsonians, who styles himself Lord High Admiral, and are confident of being paid."

The Great Sandjanum remained sceptical.

"Confident of how much?"

Adeodatus had to hesitate yet again.

"As I said, they are very unorthodox in the way they do things. Maybe it is because they have been away so long. They claim that they are to be paid ten thousand gold doubloons."

The Great Sandjanum could not suppress a snort of derision.

"Doubloons? What in the Galaxy are doubloons? Why can't these buffoons use real money like everyone else?"

"I sympathize, but gold is always real money," replied Adeodatus, "and ten thousand of anything in gold has to be a lot of real money."

The Great Sandjanum snorted again.

"Well, we will want at least half, depending on what these doubloon things are worth."

It was Adeodatus' turn to express derision.

"We couldn't possibly offer more than a quarter."

They glared at each other across the table, each knowing that they would settle on a third. It was time to seal the deal.

"May the one true God shine his benevolence on you and all your followers," said Adeodatus.

"May the Supreme Qudai shower his blessings on you and all your followers," replied the Great Sandjanum.

7

The carriage swayed as it trundled over the uneven road and the driver gave an occasional pull on the reins to check the donkey. Jim breathed deeply and gazed at the passing landscape as the air streamed past his face.

"I must say, this is a most pleasant way to get about," said de la Beche. "So much nicer than all the other vehicles I've been in. You're there in a flash. Never any time to enjoy the scenery. Such a good idea of Squire Squire to take a cab – even if he was a bit sniffy about our going to see the Great Sandjanum."

"Absolutely, Sechy," agreed Doctor Culpepper. "This is much the nicest way to travel, but Squire Squire did say we needed to be careful. He didn't trust the Qwezellarans."

"I don't entirely trust anybody, Sawbones, including Squire Squire. I don't think much harm will come from a quick visit. And they did ask to see us, with a hint about the Kwokkah."

"You going to see the Great Sandjanum, Gov?" said the driver, as he gave a light frisk of his whip across the donkey's rear.

"We are indeed, darling," said de la Beche. "Do you know him?"

"I've had him in the back of my cab once or twice," came the reply.

"Really! What did you make of him?"

"He don't say much. He don't tip much neither. In fact, he don't tip at all. I've had them all in the back of my cab, one time or another. None of them big tippers. Not one."

"By 'them', I assume you mean religious leaders?" said de la Beche.

"Exactly, Gov. They're all big on the goodwill talk, but not so big on putting it into action, if you know what I mean. Mind you," he added, "they do tell me things they wouldn't tell anyone else."

Jim saw de la Beche give a start of interest.

"Is that so? What do they reveal to you?"

The driver shook his head vigorously.

"Oh, I couldn't tell you, Gov. What's said in the cab, stays in the cab. That's the Seal of the Cab, that is, as any cabbie would tell you. I'd never get another fare if I told."

They came to a gigantic building, clad in white marble, with a dome surrounded by a number of tall, thin towers.

"That's it: the Grand Kalaba," said the cabbie.

De la Beche thrust a note into his hand.

"Keep the change."

The cabbie looked at his hand and grinned.

"Thanks a lot, Gov. Do you want me to wait?"

De la Beche thought for a moment.

"I'm not sure how long we will be."

"No problem, Gov. I haven't got another fare at the moment."

"In that case, please do."

They ascended the wide steps up to the Grand Kalaba. The entrance was surrounded by intricately-carved geometric patterns in marble that reminded Jim of graphic puzzles that he had seen. De la Beche was wearing "something simple": a long, white, silk dress, decorated with gold embroidery at the neck and cuffs, and a white headdress with a tail that ran down his back.

They were met at the top by two attendants, dressed in white robes and turbans.

"Are we to be welcoming the renowned Captain de la Beche?" said one, bowing deeply.

De la Beche smiled graciously.

"Too kind, darling. Allow me introduce my companions, the equally renowned Doctor Cuthbert Culpepper and Jim, the cabin boy, who I'm sure will be renowned one day."

"Please to be welcoming Doctor Cuthbert Culpepper and Jim the cabin boy," said the other attendant, bowing equally deeply.

"You are here to be seeing the Great Sandjanum," said the first.

"If you please," said de la Beche. "Could you take us to him?"

"He is at this very moment sermoning, but soon he will be finishing. You may be entering."

They went into the Grand Kalaba. Inside it was one enormous room, its high roof supported by myriad arches. It was filled with what looked to Jim like hundreds of worshippers, moving in unison. Sometimes they were standing, sometimes kneeling, at other times prostrate on the floor. Jim watched, fascinated. It reminded him of a callisthenics display. At the far end, he saw a portly, bearded figure that he took to be the Great Sandjanum, intoning in a loud, sonorous voice. Jim tried to catch the words.

"He is talking in Ancient Candabran," said the first turban. "It is the language they are speaking in Heaven."

"Is that so? I suppose I will have to brush up on it if I want to go," mused de la Beche.

The sermon finished and the worshippers rapidly dispersed. Soon only the Great Sandjanum was left. The turbans led the three to him.

"I am introducing to you, O Great Sandjanum, the renowned Captain de la Beche, the renowned Doctor Cuthbert Culpepper and the not-yet-renowned Jim, the cabin boy," said turban number one.

The Great Sandjanum opened both arms wide.

"Welcome, welcome, Captain de la Beche and Doctor Cuthbert Culpepper and Jim, the cabin boy. We have heard you are on a holy mission. What can we do for you?"

De la Beche put on what Jim recognized as his ingratiating face.

"So grateful that you could meet us, Your Great Sandjanimity. Allow me to congratulate you on this magnificent Grand Kalaba."

The Great Sandjanum nodded.

"We are servants of the all-mighty, the all-benevolent, the all-knowing Qudai. All blessings to Him. He leads us into righteousness and punishes all sins and transgressions. He sends death to the thief and the murderer, to the adulterer and the fornicator, to the infidel and the apostate and to all who reject His holy word."

"I did hear that he is not too easy to please," said de la Beche, "but I'm sure in the case of the Grand Kalaba, he is absolutely delighted."

"He bestows eternal blessings on all His sons who are faithful to Him in all manner of things. Ask of Him and you will surely receive."

"I'm very glad to hear it, Your Great Sandjanimity. As you may know, we are seeking the whereabouts of a sacred vessel, the Holy Kwokkah. We had heard that you were willing to help us."

The Great Sandjanum smiled benevolently.

"Ah yes, of course, the Kwokkah. Whether it is holy is a question. Who is it that venerates this object?"

"I believe they are called the Nullarboreans."

Jim watched as the Great Sandjanum appeared, literally, to be chewing this over, his jaw moving slowly from side to side.

"They have never come to my attention. Do they worship the one true deity, whose name it is beyond the power of mere mortals to understand?"

"I'm afraid I'm not absolutely familiar with all their practices," replied de la Beche, "but I am assured that they are a very god-worshipping bunch. Always at it, so I'm told."

Jim saw the Great Sandjanum give this more masticatory consideration.

"There are those who can convince themselves in the righteousness of their belief, though they be in the greatest error. Perhaps we should send a mission to them. The Holy Warriors of the Almighty can be most persuasive."

"I'm sure they would be most welcome, Your Great Sandjanimity. If you wish, I will put in a good word with some people I know in their neighbourhood."

The Great Sandjanum nodded.

"That would be very good of you. As for the Kwokkah, we may soon have some good news for you. But first, this is the feast of Orkombo, commemorating the time when our most holy prophet, Monstifi, all benevolence be upon him, in the first days of his holy mission, went forth with his band of followers, great blessings be upon them, and slew all the males of the infidel city, Zagoim, and took into slavery their wives and daughters. There is feasting and music and dancing. You will enjoy."

He motioned them to sit on some cushions at the side of the room. Almost immediately, many of the worshippers returned and began decorating the room with bunting and flowers. The air became heavy with the scent of burning joss sticks and candles. Musicians appeared with their instruments and began playing. Jim found himself caught up in the insistent, repetitive, mystical rhythms, almost as if he was being transported out of his body.

The music gradually became louder and faster. Out of a side door stepped a troupe of veiled dancers, who began weaving fantastic, whirling patterns. As he watched the lithe bodies pirouette across the floor, trailing multi-coloured veils, Jim became aware that, what at first he had assumed were youthful males, looked more and more as if they were female. He looked more closely and became almost convinced that they were female.

Jim glanced at his companions. Doctor Culpepper was staring at the dancers as if transfixed and Jim thought he also saw a faint look of puzzlement on the face of de la Beche. A few moments later, the Great Sandjanum came over to them.

"Food and drink will be served soon. Are you enjoying the dancing?"

"Absolutely, Your Great Sandjanimity. Almost sublime," replied de la Beche.

"It is a re-enactment of the time when the wives and daughters of the Zagoimites were released from their infidel husbands and fathers and given to the believers of the true God, Qudai," said the Great Sandjanum. "It is one of our most sacred dances."

"Ah yes, I can see it now. Most touching," said de la Beche, "And the dancers make such convincing females."

"They are slaves, Captain de la Beche. To re-enact the event, they must be slaves," said the Great Sandjanum.

Jim saw de la Beche show only a fleeting moment of surprise.

"Of course – and, as I said, most convincing."

"They are convincing, Captain de la Beche," said the Great Sandjanum, "because they are female slaves."

This time, de la Beche could not hide his surprise.

"I thought females were not allowed to be on Utrophia, Your Great Sandjanimity?"

"That is true, Captain de la Beche," replied the Great Sandjanum. "The Treaty of Opiuchus forbids female *persons* to come to Utrophia, but, in our religion, slaves are not considered persons. They are *chattels*. The Treaty of Opiuchus allows us to bring any goods and chattels to Utrophia that we require for our religious observance."

"Slaves are required for religious observance?"

"Yes, of course, as you see in our sacred dance."

"And are they required for anything else?"

The Great Sandjanum shrugged.

"We are not against pleasure, Captain de la Beche."

Food and drink arrived as the music and dancing continued. Jim had been sipping a particularly delicious and intoxicating concoction and found himself almost floating away in the whirl of sound and vision. He noticed the portly figure of the Great Sandjanum looming into view again.

"Is there anything else you would like, Captain?"

"As a matter of fact, there is one thing, Your Great Sandjanimity," replied de la Beche. "I was hoping that we might be able to talk about the Kwokkah and how you might help us find it."

The Great Sandjanum smiled.

"All in good time, Captain. This is the feast of Orkombo, a time for rejoicing in the defeat of the Zagoimites. We will discuss the matter soon."

"I quite understand," said de la Beche. "Perhaps we should leave now and come back another time?"

Jim saw the trace of a frown appear on the Great Sandjanum's face.

"Are you not enjoying our hospitality, Captain de la Beche?"

"Of course we are, Your Great Sandjanimity. We have rarely enjoyed finer, but we don't want to overstay our welcome. Besides, we don't want to keep our cabbie waiting too long."

The Great Sandjanum waved his hand dismissively.

"Do not worry about the cab driver, Captain. I am pleased that you are enjoying your time with us. I have arranged accommodation for you and your companions here."

De la Beche hesitated before replying.

"I beg your pardon, Your Great Sandjanimity, but I thought you said something about accommodation."

"Of course, Captain. We always treat our guests well."

"That's very kind of you, I'm sure, but we do need to get back. We have work to do."

Jim felt a twinge of alarm at this turn of events, but the Great Sandjanum's expression remained blandly benign.

"I am afraid I could not possibly allow it, Captain. As you see, night has fallen and it is not safe for you to travel. Our gates are closed at night and cannot be opened until morning. I could never forgive myself if something happened to you and your companions. Our religion enjoins us to offer hospitality and protection to all travellers, so do not worry yourselves. In the meantime, there is much more feasting and music to come. Please, enjoy yourselves."

8

Commander Splenditheran looked at the new Chief of Staff seated opposite and felt a mounting sense of *déjà vu*. Chiefs of Staff to the commanders of the Southern Cross Federation had traditionally come from the military; the new appointment was no exception. Some fancied themselves as intellectuals and would expound upon the philosophy of conflict and the finer points of military strategy. Others tended to be of a more robust turn of mind and would say that the answer to any and all questions was the unlimited and overwhelming use of force. Splenditheran was beginning to think that the new appointment was firmly in the latter camp.

The Nullarborean situation was becoming worse by the day and his handling of it was being criticized from all sides. It was not just the Nullarboreans and their unfathomable religiosity. Instability was spreading. Disaffection was being reported on a number of planets in the Federation, with threats of secession. One planet even wanted to join the Arcturan Empire because, as its leader was reported to have said, "The parties would be better."

His options were limited. If de la Beche succeeded in retrieving the Kwokkah, then that at least would give him something with which to soothe the Nullarborean distemper, which was at the root of his troubles. He decided to broach the matter with the Chief of Staff.

"What is the latest news on the Nullarborean situation?"

The Chief of Staff snorted.

"The Nullarboreans are full of shit."

That, thought Splenditheran, might well be true, but it was not what he had asked. He tried again.

"Have your spies come up with anything that might indicate that the Nullarboreans might defect to the Orsonians?"

The Chief of Staff snorted again. Those spies had been recruited by his predecessor, whose traitorous carcase had since been dissociated into its constituent atoms.

"The spies are full of shit. They never tell us anything worth knowing."

Splenditheran suspected that might be true as well, but it was not helping matters.

"I need to brief you on a particularly sensitive matter. This discussion must be kept absolutely secret. Have you heard of the Holy Kwokkah, a vessel sacred to the Nullarboreans?"

The Chief of Staff made a gruff sound that Splenditheran took as a no.

"It was believed lost, but the Orsonians convinced the Nullarboreans that they had it, or at least knew where it was, and would tell them if they defected."

"The Orsonians are full of shit."

Splenditheran knew that was certainly true, but it was beside the point.

"Have you heard of Captain de la Beche of HMS *Bountiful*, the privateer?"

"Rings a bell. He's full of shit. Dresses all girlie, doesn't he?"

"He can be a little unorthodox, but that is the advantage. He is able to operate in any jurisdiction, so I have asked him to re-cover the Kwokkah. We can then return it to the Nullarboreans and, in their gratitude, they will forget the idea of defecting."

The Chief of Staff frowned sceptically. That sounded a bit too neat.

"*Has* he got it?"

"We are not sure. Have you heard of the Planet Utrophia?"

The Chief of Staff snorted again.

"They're all full of shit there, so they tell me."

Splenditheran decided to ignore the remark.

"We believe that the Kwokkah is somewhere on the planet and de la Beche is there trying to find it. We need to contact him to see what progress he has made."

The Chief of Staff shrugged.

"Don't ask me to do it. You need one of the godly lot."

Splenditheran stared at him in frustration.

"But surely, with all your clandestine techniques, you should be able to contact him?"

The Chief of Staff shook his head.

"Nope. No can do. Everything gets blocked unless it's from one of our god-fearing brethren. If you want my advice," he added, "I would go there and blast the lot. Someone would squeal and tell you where the kwokking thing is."

Splenditheran thought it best to ignore the advice.

"In that case, we had better consult the High Sapient."

The High Sapient entered and gazed with faint distaste at Splenditheran's magnificent inner chamber, with its murals and artworks. The High Sapient considered himself an ascetic and valued things of the spirit above all.

"You asked to see me, Commander?"

"I did indeed, Your Most Cerebral Intelligence. As I was explaining to the Chief of Staff, we are engaged upon a most sensitive and delicate mission and we need to be in contact with someone on the planet Utrophia. As you know we of the, er," he hesitated, searching for the word, "secular world, cannot do so. We were hoping you might be able to help us."

The High Sapient looked at Splenditheran as if he had gone slightly mad.

"That would not be possible, Commander. If you remember, we no longer have any communication with Utrophia."

Splenditheran looked at him, bemused.

"No, I do not remember. What is the problem?"

The High Sapient's already low opinion of the sanity of the secular world sank further.

"Over two centuries ago, a number of sects on Utrophia, most unusually, set aside their mutual antagonism and banded together to excommunicate the Non-Inflationary Denomination of the Sacrosanctity of Reason. They declared that a belief in the laws of physics and the rationality of existence under the Supreme Ineffability is incompatible with Faith and therefore that the Non-Inflationary Denomination of the Sacrosanctity of Reason is not a religion as defined under the Treaty of Opiuchus. Naturally, we challenged this declaration, but the court adjudicating was entirely comprised of members of the same sects that had made the declaration, so our challenge failed. Consequently, we can no longer communicate with Utrophia. We have appealed, although no date for an appeal hearing has been set."

Splenditheran stared at him, as if not quite believing what he had heard.

"There is no possibility of contacting Utrophia?"

"None whatsoever, Commander."

Splenditheran continued to stare at him for several seconds before finally speaking.

"Thank you, Your Most Cerebral Intelligence. That will be all."

They watched as the High Sapient left.

"What did I tell you?" said the Chief of Staff. "Full of shit."

9

Jim awoke and looked around the room. He still had an uneasy feeling as he remembered the events of the previous night. A turbanned one had led them into their suite, accompanied by two uniformed flunkeys carrying trays of food and drink that they placed on a table.

"Please be making yourself comfortable," the flunkey said, pointing to an object on the wall. "If you are needing any assistance, please be pressing this button."

"Thank you, darling." said de la Beche. "Wouldn't it be better to contact you with something more, ah, serviceable, like a communicator?"

The turbanned one had looked a little surprised.

"Such things are not being allowed in the Grand Kalaba," and then, bowing, "for your privacy and safety, the door will be being locked for the duration of the night. Please be sleeping well."

Even though he was tired, Jim slept only fitfully. As light returned, he rose from his bed, dressed and went into the main room of the suite. De la Beche and Culpepper seemed to be still asleep. He tried the door, but it was still locked, although the food and drink on the table were different. The sight of food made him realize that he was hungry, so he sat down and began to eat. A few minutes later, he heard sounds; first Doctor Culpepper and then de la Beche emerged from their rooms. De la Beche's outfit looked distinctly less pristine and his makeup had barely survived the night. They both sat down and joined Jim in his breakfast.

"Now, darlings," said de la Beche, wiping crumbs from his mouth, "let us make our departure."

He tried the door and found, like Jim, that it was still locked, so he went to the wall and pressed the button. Nothing happened; he pressed it again, several times.

Eventually, the door opened and the turbanned one from the previous night appeared.

"You are requesting some assistance?"

"Not at all, darling," said de la Beche. "We simply want to leave. Please show us the way out."

The turbanned one seemed to be a little flustered.

"You must not be leaving until the Great Sandjanum has been speaking with you."

"Always delighted to talk to His Great Sandjanimity," replied de la Beche. "Where is he?"

The turbanned one became more flustered.

"He will be being here very presently."

He shut the door; when de la Beche tried it, it was locked.

An hour later, the door opened and the Great Sandjanum swept into the room.

"Captain de la Beche, so good to see you again. I hope you have been comfortable?"

"I am not complaining about the service, Your Great Sand-janimity, but I would like to know why we should be locked up in here?"

The Great Sandjanum's face took on an expression of concern.

"My apologies for the inconvenience, Captain, but I assure you that it is for your own safety. We have been receiving some very concerning reports that you are in great danger."

"Really? What sort of danger?"

"Danger from the Sempiternal Ecclesia, infidels of the worst possible stripe. Apparently, some of their long-lost brethren have returned and want to take you prisoner, for what purpose, I hesitate to imagine."

De la Beche looked at him sceptically

"That sounds most unlikely. I have never had anything to do with the Sempiternal Ecclesia. Who are these long-lost brethren?"

"I only have their names, Captain. They are called Reverend Jonah, Reverend Maggie and Reverend Dick, but I can assure you that, even now, agents of the Sempiternal Ecclesia are looking everywhere for you."

The three looked at each other.

"Sloakum!" said Doctor Culpepper. "How did he get here?"

"Even more to the point," said de la Beche, "how did he persuade the Sempiternal Ecclesia that he was one of their long-lost brethren? I don't think anyone would give him top marks for piety."

The Great Sandjanum showed even more concern.

"You know of them, Captain?"

"Unfortunately, we do, although you needn't worry about us. We can deal with them."

The Great Sandjanum shook his head.

"You are under my care, Captain. The rules of our religion require that I cannot let you leave here until I am completely sure that you will be safe. I would be damned for all eternity if I allowed you to be put in any danger. You will be very comfortable, but we must keep you here until we have dealt with the infidel Sempiternal Ecclesia. I can assure you that it will not take very long. We have dealt with them before. I shall leave you now, but I expect to return soon with good news for you about the object you seek, the, ah, …"

"Kwokkah," said Jim, before he could stop himself.

"Exactly; the Kwokkah. For the moment, make yourself at home and call for anything that you need."

Jim watched as the Great Sandjanum and his retainers left the room.

"I'm beginning to smell a rat, Sechy," said Doctor Culpepper.

"Quite so, Sawbones. Excessive hospitality is always a hostile act in my experience. I don't believe this rubbish about protecting us. We know Sloakum is after us. I suspect that this lot are in cahoots with him and these Sempiternal creatures. They're planning to sell us to them." He fished out his communicator from a hidden pocket, flipped the prayer book leaf and stared at the screen. "Completely dead. As they said, no technology works here. It looks like we will have to find a way out on our own."

10

Sloakum, Maggie and McGoon were ushered into the presence of the Ecclesiarch. Adeodatus smiled benignly on them.

"Reverends Jonah, Maggie and Dick, I have good news for you. We have located the heretic, de la Beche."

Sloakum chortled and Maggie clapped her hands.

"Thankee, Yer Worship," said Sloakum. "If ye'll be so good as to hand him over to us, we will see to it that he gets his just deserts."

Adeodatus hesitated. Maggie noticed that there was a slight edge to his benign expression.

"There are one or two issues that need to be addressed before we can proceed. De la Beche is not yet in our hands. He is being held by the Qwezellarans in that preposterous edifice they call the Grand Kalaba."

Maggie, Sloakum and Dick looked back at him blankly.

"I see they are not known to you. The Qwezellarans are infidels of the worst sort. They worship the false god Qudai, who apparently demands that they indulge in all sorts of licentious and idolatrous behaviour."

Sloakum gave what he thought was a disapproving tut.

"Then we'd better get him out of there, Yer Worship. He's got enough bad ideas already, without him getting any more."

A suspicion dawned on Maggie.

"Why are they holding him, Yer Worship?"

The Ecclesiarch sat back in his throne.

"There's the rub, Reverends. The Qwezellarans learnt somehow that we were seeking him. I'm afraid little remains secret forever on Utrophia. They have discovered, too, that there is a considerable bounty on his head, which you hope to collect."

His head leant forward and he stared at them keenly. They exchanged uneasy glances.

"Bounty, what bounty?" said Maggie.

"They believe that you have been commissioned to capture de la Beche by others, who will pay you when you turn him over to them. Is that true?"

"Well, they did say they would pay our expenses," said Sloakum.

"May I ask who *they* are?" said Adeodatus.

The three exchanged more glances.

"The Orsonians," said Maggie, finally.

"The Orsonians," repeated Adeodatus. "Another cabal for whom the word infidel does not begin to do justice. The expenses that you say you would incur seem to be very considerable – and all to be paid in gold, I understand."

"That's right, Yer Worship," said Sloakum. "We like to get paid in gold. We don't like any of that funny money. And ye must like it too, I see," he added, looking around. "Plenty of gold here."

"Indeed, Reverend Jonah," said the Ecclesiarch. "We use gold to celebrate the glory of the one true God. Unfortunately, the Qwezellarans are also partial to gold for use in their idolatrous practices – and that brings me to a second issue."

"It does?" asked Maggie.

"Indeed it does. I know, as Alcocatamites and followers of the one true God, that you are familiar with your obligation of terces."

He gave them a meaningful look.

"In which," he continued, "you are obliged to give a third of all you earn and possess to God's holy church, the Sempiternal Ecclesia."

A shock seemed to reverberate through Sloakum's frame. Maggie's face froze, while McGoon gawked, open-mouthed. Adeodatus appeared not to notice their reaction.

"Normally that would leave you with two-thirds of the proceeds, which ought to be enough for you to continue your sacred ministry."

"What do ye mean, 'normally'?" growled Sloakum, struggling to regain his composure.

"Unfortunately," replied the Ecclesiarch, "the Qwezellarans, known throughout the Galaxy for their greed and covetousness, have proved once again true to their nature. They are demanding half of any ransom paid to you before releasing de la Beche."

Sloakum exploded in spittle-flecked fury.

"I'll slit every one of their scurvy gizzards. I'll feed their innards to the crows. That pack of double-crossing bilge rats will rue the day they ever heard of Jonah Sloakum."

Adeodatus stepped out of sputum range.

"Your anger is understandable, Reverend Jonah, but it is a little unbecoming to your holy status. A period of quiet reflection is in order, to allow us to consider what we do next."

"Ye say they want paying upfront, before they let him go," said Maggie, "but we won't get paid until we hand him over to the Orsonians. So what'll we pay them with?"

Adeodatus nodded. "That is indeed a conundrum. Fortunately, I think that we can persuade them to wait for their reward."

Sloakum was still grumblinglike a rumbling volcano; McGoon seemed catatonic. Maggie was doubtful.

"How do we know they won't have him burned up and blowed up, like that one ye done?"

Adeodatus seemed a little pained by her question.

"That was the just punishment for heresy, as ordained by the one true religion. Infidels like the Qwezellarans have only avarice as their guiding principle. They will wait, if they think the prize is worth it."

Maggie sensed that Sloakum was about to suggest a few ideas for persuading them. She held him back.

"What d'ye think might convince them, Yer Worship?"

Adeodatus paused before answering.

"First, they must be certain that the reward is real. You will need a notarized affidavit to that effect, signed by both the highest temporal and religious authorities on Orson."

Sloakum's inner volcano began rumbling again.

"Maybe we could go and talk to them, beat them down a bit?" suggested Maggie.

"I'm afraid that will not be possible," replied Adeodatus. "Such negotiations can only take place between religious authorities on Utrophia. It is part of the Treaty. We will have your best interests at heart and will handle everything on your behalf."

"Will that cost us?" asked Maggie.

"Of course not," said Adeodatus. "It is our religious duty."

"So we won't have to pay this third of all we've got, like ye were talking about?"

The Ecclesiarch looked at her quizzically.

"Terces is the religious obligation of all who serve the one true faith. As members of the sacred Alcocatamites, I cannot imagine that you would refuse to honour terces, but, if you did, you would be repudiating the faith. You would in effect be declaring yourselves heretics – and you have seen what happens to heretics."

Maggie could feel that Sloakum's inner volcano was about to erupt. She decided to play for time.

"We wouldn't want to do nothing wrong, Yer Worship. We'll have to think about things and, as ye say, contact the Orsonians to see if they'll agree to pay a bit up front."

The Ecclesiarch smiled benignly.

"Of course. We on our side will pray for your success. Perhaps I can remind you that mortification of the flesh is the surest way of achieving a happy outcome and my offer of a chaplain to administer your cat o' nine tails is always open. Say the word, and I will order it."

"Very kind of ye, I'm sure, Yer Worship, but I think we can wait a bit on that one," replied Maggie. "Let's see what the Orsonians say first."

***

"I told you no good would come of it if we came here. Let's get out now, while we can."

Dick McGoon had had enough. "It was bad enough last time with all them mad monks. The way things are going, we'll be rumbled and next thing we know, we'll be burned up and blowed to bits."

They had gone back to their quarters. Sloakum was spluttering incoherently, while Maggie gazed, mute, out of a window.

"And if we stay, what's it for?" continued McGoon. "This lot will take a third, the other lot want a third or maybe a half and we'll be left with a pittance. That's if the Orsonians cough up – and I don't see that happening."

Maggie had to agree.

"Dick's right, Jonah Sloakum. This is all your doing, so what do ye say we do next?"

Slaokum began to foam at the mouth.

"How do they know about the gold? Who snitched on us? I'll have his guts hanging from the bowsprit when I find him."

Maggie gave him a withering look.

"Ye told them, Jonah Sloakum. Ye were always going on when we were alone about what ye were going to do with the gold. They must have been listening in. That'll teach ye to keep yer mouth shut."

Sloakum's splutterings rose to a crescendo.

"I say we tell this lot to go hang. I'll give 'em cat o' nine tails. That'll make 'em pray good and hard. We'll bring some of the crew down and we'll find these Qwezzies. They'll give us Fancypants, if they know what's good for 'em, and we won't pay a penny."

Maggie snorted.

"That bunch of drunken good-fer-nothings ye call a crew couldn't frighten a mouse, Jonah Sloakum. Remember, their weapons don't work down here. One whiff of cold steel and they're cacking their pants. We have to play this canny. We'll go along with it fer now, but I'm with Dick. If all we're ever going to get out of it is crumbs, then we get out and think of something else."

"All I'm thinking," said Sloakum, "is that I want them ten thousand gold doubloons. I ain't going to take a penny less."

There was silence for a while, and then Maggie spoke.

"Yer right, Jonah Sloakum, ten thousand it has to be. But it looks like we're going to have to pay a ransom, so ye'll have to go back to his Lord High Admiralship and tell him it's going to cost him more if he wants Fancypants. Fifteen thousand should do it."

Sloakum's expression was part snarl, part sneer.

"What good will that do? His high and mighty greedyguts Worship will be wanting half of it."

Maggie shook her head.

"We're finished with him. We go straight to those Quezzies and do a deal."

"I thought he said they wouldn't talk to us," said McGoon. "These religious types only talk to each other."

"Have ye been keeping yer eyes shut, Dick McGoon?" said Maggie, derisively. "There's gold everywhere here. They say it's fer their God, but it's really fer theirselves. That's religious types for ye – keep theirselves in every form of comfort. I bet the Qwezzies are no different. His Worship said as much. We offer them bagfuls of gold and they'll bite our hands off."

11

Junipa gazed disconsolately at the desolate surface of Utrophia and began to have second thoughts.

She recalled vividly the last conversation she had with Orestia.

"Disguise myself as a male? How do you imagine I could do that?"

"I don't think it will be too difficult," said Orestia, in soothing tones. "Just make sure you dress in something that covers all your body and drop your voice a tone or two. Besides, male religious types only see what they want to see."

What they would not want to see, thought Junipa, was "Samantha Disembowelling and Castrating the Destrigian, Driffix" by Gentiligia Artimesci, that now had pride of place on Orestia's wall. That, however cheering in all its gore, was no help. Junipa looked at her, unconvinced.

"What am I supposed to do there? We have no contacts there, nothing to go on."

"True, we don't have any contacts," replied Orestia, "but we have had information, that we can't yet verify, that there may be other females on Utrophia."

Junipa's scepticism increased.

"How can that be? I thought you said females were not allowed to go there?"

"It appears," replied Orestia, "that a particularly reactionary bunch of bigots on a planet called Qwezellar still practise slavery. As far as they are concerned, slaves are property and any property can be taken to Utrophia. Female slaves are taken there – and you can imagine why."

It took a few seconds for Junipa to control her astonishment and anger.

"That's appalling! But how does it help us?"

"Good question, especially since we can't be sure whether it is true or not. However, I can't imagine that, if there are slaves there, they are exactly happy about their situation. I'm also sure that they will know what is going on. If you could make contact with them and stir a little dissatisfaction, you might learn something. It's not a lot to go on, I admit, but it's a start."

Junipa shook her head.

"Absolutely right, it's not a lot to go on. Can't we find out more? Do we have any supporters on Qwezellar?"

"Some, but we hear hardly anything from them. Males have a total grip on all forms of communication. I have the first report here that claimed that slaves had been sent to Utrophia. It says they have gone to something called the Grand Kalaba, whatever that might be."

***

Junipa loathed all forms of religion. Was it really worth going there? What could she ever find out? Then, duty called. She swallowed her misgivings and ordered the transport to descend.

They had chosen a landing spot a little way out of what looked like a village. Small, low buildings were arranged around a square. Junipa was wearing a long, grey coat that reached almost to the ground, and a cowl pulled over her head. A scarf covered the lower part of her face and left only her eyes and nose visible. She watched the cutter depart and then turned and trudged towards the buildings. As she entered the square she saw a line of figures moving rhythmically, ringing small bells, banging on drums and chanting something that sounded like "Isbara balabasa".

She walked up to them and held her hand upright in salutation. They stopped, but continued to chant in sing-song fashion.

"Isbara balabasa, isbara balabasa, isbara balabasa."

She had no idea what that meant, so she thought she would try a question.

"Have any of you heard of something called the Grand Kalaba?"

The chanting stopped and then the leading figure said, "Isbara balabasa."

"I'm sorry. I don't understand," said Junipa.

"You have to say 'Isbara balabasa'," came the reply. "It means 'God is all'."

Junipa had to suppress a laugh at the absurdity of theclaim. But, on the other hand, why not humour him?

"Oh, very well. 'Isbara balabasa'."

He pointed to a road out of the square.

"The Grand Kalaba is several leagues from here. That's the road you need to take."

She looked along the road, which disappeared over a distant hill, but could see nothing.

"It is a long walk. Perhaps you should take a cab."

It had not occurred to Junipa that there might be cabs on Utrophia, but, if there were, they were preferable to a long walk.

"Where would I get a cab?"

He pointed to the corner of the square. All she could see was some sort of animal standing in front of a cart.

"I can only see an animal?"

He looked at her as if he thought she might be a bit dim.

"It's a donkey. It pulls the cab. You sit in it."

Junipa disliked animals. She just about tolerated the smaller sort – dogs and cats – but hated anything larger, because of their heft and their smell and their dirt. On the other hand, she disliked long walks just as much.

She walked over to where the donkey and cart stood.

The cabbie smiled at her.

"Where to, Gov?"

For a moment she was taken aback at the question, but then remembered that she was supposed to be male.

"Do you know the Grand Kalaba?"

"Yeah, 'course I do. Hop in."

Junipa had never travelled in anything drawn by an animal, but as they trundled along the road she found the experience surprisingly pleasant, as long as the wind did not waft the smell of the donkey in her direction.

"You going to see the Great Sandjanum?"

Junipa had no idea what he was talking about.

"Pardon?"

"The Great Sandjanum. He's the Big Cheese of the Grand Kalaba. Are you going to see him?"

"No, no. I just want to take a look at it."

"Yeah, it's quite a sight is the Grand Kalaba. I took a fare there yesterday. Three of them. They told me to wait while they had a look round, but they never came back. Good tippers, though."

Junipa never had much time for male hard luck stories. She tried to keep her eyes on the landscape as they drove, but the cabbie carried on chatting.

"Odd lot they were. Their governor was quite a sight. All dressed up very fancy. Long white thing with lots of gold and a great big hat. Lots of airs about him. Then there was an old geezer with a moustache and the third one couldn't have been much more than a boy."

Junipa was startled. That had to be more than a coincidence.

"This governor, as you call him, did he have a very flamboyant manner, perhaps call you 'darling'?"

The cabbie looked at her in surprise.

"As a matter of fact, he did. Do you know him?"

"Yes I do. Do you know where he is now?"

The cabbie shook his head.

"No idea. As I said, he went into the Grand Kalaba, but I never saw him come out, even though he told me to wait for him. In the end, one of their flunkeys told me he wasn't coming out. Maybe he's still there."

Junipa paid off the cabbie with what she thought was an adequate tip and said she didn't need him to wait. Getting into the Grand Kalaba was even more urgent now that she knew de la Beche had been there and perhaps still was. She ascended the stairs in front of the building and pretended to look at its facade, which even she had to admit was magnificent. She watched as a person approached the entrance and was stopped by an attendant. He started bowing rhythmically, reciting something that she took to be a sacred text. She moved closer and heard the attendant ask him what were the five obligations of the faithful. She couldn't catch the mumbled reply, but they appeared to satisfy the attendant, because he was allowed to enter. Over the next few minutes she saw several others go through the same routine. Entering the Grand Kalaba through the main entrance, she concluded, was not going to be easy.

She decided to try another tack and started to walk round the perimeter of the massive building. It was entirely surrounded by high, spike-tipped, iron railings, impossible to climb over. The only gap appeared to be two iron gates at the rear. She examined them, but there was no obvious way in which they might be opened. Just as she was about to move on, the gates swung open and a figure pushing a large, wheeled bin emerged. The bin was obviously heavy, because she could see pushing it took a lot of effort. Suddenly, a wheel snagged on a raised paving stone and the bin swung round. The pusher pitched forward, banging his head hard on the side of the bin and falling on the ground, blood coming from a cut on his forehead.

She rushed over to see how he was. He was sitting, dazed, on the ground, holding his hand to his head. She could see blood trickling through his fingers. She took a kerchief from her pocket, took his hand away and held the kerchief to the wound.

"Hold it there. The cut's not too bad. It should stop bleeding in a few minutes."

He sat there for several minutes, still dazed. Eventually he managed to get unsteadily to his feet, but fell down again, clutching his leg.

"Have you hurt your leg as well?" asked Junipa.

"Yes," he said, grimacing and rubbing the affected limb.

"Let me have a look," she said and began examining the leg. "I don't think anything is broken. Just sit there for a while."

He gave her a grateful smile. Junipa looked around and realized that this could be a way to get into the Grand Kalaba.

"What do you want done with the bin?"

"Leave it there. It's for the hermits and holy beggars."

"Pardon?" said Junipa.

"It's food left over from the feast of Orkombo. We leave it for the hermits and holy beggars. They have to eat too."

"I suppose they do," said Junipa. "Is the leg any better?"

"A little," he said and rose to his feet, just managing to stay upright. "I have to go back now."

"Let me help you," said Junipa. "Take my arm."

"Thanks," he said, giving her a grateful smile and started hobbling back, leaning heavily on Junipa's arm. "My name is Nimbolt. What's yours?"

Stupidly, thought Junipa, she had not thought of a male name for herself. She said the first thing that came into her mind.

"Gruff."

He looked amused.

"You don't sound very gruff."

"What has that to do with it? I might just as well ask what Nimbolt means."

"He was the general who conquered the empire of the Yoanites for Qudai."

"Was he? And how many empires have you conquered?"

Junipa noticed a look of sadness appear on his face.

"Nimbolt is not my real name. It is the name I must use."

Junipa looked at him perplexed.

"What do you mean, the name that you must use?"

"It is the name given to me by my masters. I am a slave, you see."

Nimbolt nodded to a guard on the gates. They went through and the gates clanged shut after them. She helped him walk in the direction of the main building.

"Are there many slaves like you here?"

"Yes, many like me, and some not like me."

"Not like you? How?"

Nimbolt looked at her a little warily.

"I cannot speak about them. Please do not ask me."

He pointed to steps leading under the Grand Kalaba. She helped him down and through a door into what looked like a large kitchen in which several otherfigures could be seen scurrying about. They found a couple of chairs and sat down. Junipa looked around the kitchen, fascinated by the fast, dextrous movements of those preparing food.

"Are all these slaves?"

"Yes. No Qwezellaran would cook. They would think it was beneath them."

Slavery was clearly commonplace with the Qwezallarans and Nimbolt had admitted that there were other slaves "not like me". Maybe the information about female slaves might be true. She needed to find out more, but she also needed to tread carefully.

"What is it like being a slave?"

He looked at her, puzzled.

"What do you mean?"

"Well, are you happy being a slave?"

"It is not a question of being happy. I am a slave, that is all."

"Do you really want to be a slave always? There are many slaves here. What if all of you said you no longer wanted to be slaves?"

"They would say we had disobeyed Qudai, and the penalty for disobeying Qudai is death."

Like most of his type, thought Junipa, Qudai was not the easygoing sort of deity. There was little chance of any revolt of the kitchen slaves, all of whom she could see were male. She tried another tack.

"You said there are other slaves not like you. Are any of them here?"

"No."

"Where are they?"

"They are somewhere else."

She could see he was becoming uncomfortable, perhaps a little suspicious, but she decided to press on.

"Are they not like you because they are female?"

He began to blush and there was a slight stammer in his answer.

"I … I cannot say. We cannot talk about them."

That was confirmation enough.

"I thought females were not allowed on Utrophia."

He shook his head and sighed.

"Slaves are not persons to the Qwezallarans. Slaves are their property and they can do with them as they like."

She allowed herself a wry smile. So it was true how the Qwezallarans got round the ban on females. They bought them in as baggage. How to find them? Nimbolt was her only lead. She needed to get him on her side.

"Nimbolt, you don't want to be a slave forever, do you?"

"No."

There was nothing for it. She had to take a chance.

"Look, I can't promise anything. I may be able to help you, but first I need to contact those female slaves. Will you trust me?"

Nimbolt stared at her, mute, before finally speaking.

"I bring them food every day. I am going to them in two hours. You can come with me."

Nimbolt reached inside a locker and pulled out a red tunic, like the one he was wearing. "You will need to wear this," he said, tossing it to her. She was glad her breasts were small and did not show much under her baggy shirt, but, just in case, she turned away from him as she took off her coat and slipped the tunic on.

"Are you sure no one will see I am not one of you slaves?" asked Junipa.

"All slaves look alike to Qwezallarans. They won't notice. Take this and follow me," said Nimbolt, pointing to a large tray of cakes and sweets. He picked up two pitchers of what she assumed was some sort of cordial and they walked out of the kitchen. Junipa noticed that Nimbolt was still limping slightly as they walked across an anteroom towards stairs and started up them.

"You must be very careful if you want to talk to the females," whispered Nimbolt. "They are guarded by a slave master."

"A male slave master?" asked Junipa, whispering too.

For the first time, she saw Nimbolt grin.

"More or less. He has had certain parts removed. That's why he can be in charge of females."

Junipa found herself grinning too, as well as wishing the same fate on the rest of maledom.

"Does he guard them very carefully?"

"Yes, we will need to distract him."

"How would we do that?"

Nimbolt gave a sly smile.

"He is not without desires. He likes to talk to me."

It took a few seconds for Junipa to grasp what he had said.

"Ah. And do you like to talk to him?"

Nimbolt pulled a disgusted face.

"Of course not, but he is harmless. If he did anything he would be scourged – or worse."

At the top of the stairs were large, ornately carved and gilded doors, guarded by two liveried sentries. One of them pushed a button and the doors swung open. They entered a large, well-lit room, lined with padded sofas, on which the female slaves lounged. They were dressed in flowing, diaphanous robes that did little to hide the fact of their sex. Nimbolt motioned to Junipa to put the tray on a table in the middle of the room, placed his pitchers down and then turned and smiled at the blubbery figure of the slave master, who was sitting on a raised chair in the corner. She saw the slave master give a simpering smile in return. Nimbolt walked over to him and said something that she didn't catch. The slave master rose from his chair and the two of them went across the room and out of glass doors that opened onto a balcony, disappearing from her sight. Junipa could no longer hear them talking, so she guessed she must be out of their earshot too.

She went over to the nearest slave and sat down beside her. The slave drew back from her and moved away.

"Can I talk to you?" said Junipa in a low voice.

The slave looked startled.

"We cannot talk. It is forbidden."

Junipa decided she had to take the risk.

"I am not like the others. I am female, too."

There was a sharp intake of breath. Two of the other slaves were in hearing distance and turned their heads, half frightened, half in wonder. All three turned to look at the doors to the balcony. Nimbolt and the slave master were not visible. They turned back to Junipa. None of them said anything.

"Do you want me to prove it?" asked Junipa.

The slave gave a little nod.

Junipa drew up her tunic and shirt to show her small, pert breast.

The slave gazed at it wide eyed, then reached out a hand and touched it, tentatively. Junipa felt a frisson of pleasure.

"It is real," said the slave in amazement.

"Of course it's real," said Junipa.

The slave touched it again, as if to make sure.

"How did you get here? Why do you want to talk to us?"

Junipa hesitated. How much to reveal? As little as possible, to start. She had no idea whether she could trust these slaves.

"My name is Junipa. What is yours?"

The slave looked puzzled.

"The name they have given me is Dorinta. Why do you want to know?"

"Is Dorinta your slave name?"

Dorinta looked apprehensive.

"It is the name I was given."

"Did you have another before you were a slave?"

"I cannot talk about such things, else they say that Qudai would punish me."

"You believe in Qudai?"

"If I do not believe, they say that he will punish me more."

The tone of her voice suggested to Junipa that her belief in Qudai had more to do with self-preservation than conviction.

"If you were not a slave, would you believe in Qudai?"

There was no reply, but Junipa detected a slight smile playing about Dorinta's lips.

"How do they treat you here?"

"They say we are their property and they can do with us what they will."

This time Junipa saw no smile, but a hint of disgust in her eyes.

"Do you want to be a slave?"

Again, no reply, but the disgust was more evident. Junipa decided she needed to reveal more.

"I think your plight is dreadful. I would like to help you."

Dorinta stared, clearly unsure of what to make of Junipa's words.

"How can you help?"

"I am not from here. I come from a world where females rule. We want to help all females to be free."

Dorinta was unconvinced.

"How could we be free? Where would we go? We are watched all the time and if we tried to escape then ..." Her voice trailed off.

Junipa could hardly argue that rescue was at hand.

"I know things look hopeless right now, but one day you will be free. We will do all we can to make it happen."

Dorinta gave a half smile, as if wanting to believe, despite her doubts. Junipa pressed on.

"If you want to be free you, must act together." She turned to the two sitting near to Dorinta. "What are your names?"

"Frumeseta," said one. "Floara," replied the other.

"Do you want to escape being slaves?"

Both hesitated and then nodded.

"I am not from here. Where I have come from, we call ourselves Feminarchs. It is a planet ruled by females. We are pledged to rid the Galaxy of the domination of males and the curse of religion. We have members all over the Galaxy. Would you like to join us?"

"What do you mean, join you?" asked Dorinta. "What would we have to do?"

"At the moment you must do nothing, but you could be our eyes and ears on this planet, Utrophia. You could tell us what is happening, and we would try to find ways of rescuing you. I cannot promise anything, but we have liberated many in the past."

They looked at each other and Junipa saw them smile.

"Yes," said Frumeseta, "we will join you."

Junipa felt a surge of elation, tempered by concern as she looked at them, so young and vulnerable.

"There is one thing that you may be able to help me with now. I am trying to find an individual, a male, though he dresses in a very gaudy style and has extravagant manners. You would know who I mean if you saw him. I believe he was here very recently. Do you know anything about him?"

All three nodded.

"He was here at the feast of Orkombo when we danced," said Dorinta.

"He is still here," said Floara. "I was told that they would not let him go."

"Why would they not let him go?" said Junipa. "Do you mean he is a captive?"

"Perhaps, or maybe he wants to stay," replied Floara.

Junipa was puzzled.

"Why do they want him?"

"I do not know."

"Do you know where they are holding him?"

"No," said Floara, "but there are others with him."

12

The Lord High Admiral of the Orsonian Fleet gazed at the message. Like all communications from Utrophia, it had come through religious channels, from a sect called the Sempiternal Ecclesia, whom he had been told were pagan idol-worshippers. For a moment he felt relieved that Sloakum had finally managed to communicate and that he had tracked de la Beche down. That relief turned to a mixture of anger and exasperation when he saw the demand for more payment. What was all this about a "ransom"? Surely the whole point of engaging a brigand like Sloakum was that he wouldn't bother with the niceties of negotiations with a bunch of clerics. If he knew where de la Beche was, then he should go in and take him and leave those clerics wringing their hands and invoking the wrath of whatever false god they happened to worship.

The Admiral was beyond wrath. The whole question of gold – not to mention doubloons – had been vexing him. He still had no real idea of what a doubloon was or whether the gold was available. When a Lord High Admiral is vexed, he looks for something to blame.

"Civil Servant 21346, come in here at once."

Civil Servant 21346 had been scrutinizing the latest edition of the *Galactic Inquirer* eagerly for signs that the revolution was beginning. He could see nothing explicit, though he thought the tone of the issue was even more mocking then usual. *Organize.* He had begun to organize himself. He had decided which four of the Admiral's mistresses he would take – and which two he would confine himself to, if he had to be frugal – and how he would furnish and redecorate the Admiral's office when he was installed. *Begin, and we will contact you*. He was still waiting for the contact.

He entered the Admiral's office and saw vexation written all over his face.

"Civil Servant 21346, I have received a message from Captain Sloakum."

Civil Servant 21346 was doubly surprised; first, that the Admiral had received a message; second, that he appeared to be vexed by it. He sensed an opportunity to annoy him further.

"That is indeed good news, Lord High Admiral."

The Admiral's eyes narrowed. As ever, he could never quite decide whether Civil Servant 21346 was being wilfully aggravating.

"It is not good news, because he is demanding more payment. He now wants fifteen thousand of the things he calls doubloons – all in gold, of course."

Civil Servant 21346 was even more surprised, not to say delighted.

"Why is that, Lord High Admiral? I understood you have a contract. Surely you can hold him to it?"

The Admiral's eyes narrowed further, but he decided to continue.

"Sloakum informs me that de la Beche is being held by one of the sects on Utrophia and they are demanding a ransom for his release. The further payment is for the ransom."

Civil Servant 21346 felt another frisson of pleasure.

"Does the contract not have the standard clause stating that the contracted party pays all incidental expenses, Lord High Admiral? I would have thought a ransom would come under incidental expenses."

The Admiral's eyes had become mere slits. He knew that Civil Servant 21346 knew that there was no contract and he knew, too, that Civil Servant 21346 knew that he, the Lord High Admiral, could not admit it. All he could do was bluff it out.

"Nonsense. A ransom is a quite exceptional matter. It comes under some sort of force."

"*Force majeure,* Lord High Admiral?"

"Exactly, *force majeure.* Now, do we have another five thousand doubloons?"

"That depends on what you mean, Lord High Admiral."

The Admiral could no longer hide his annoyance.

"What do you mean by what do I mean, Civil Servant 21346? I mean, do we have five thousand more doubloons?"

"I'm sorry, Lord High Admiral, I didn't make myself clear. It depends on what you mean by doubloons. I have been researching the matter, as you requested, and I'm afraid there seems to be very little information on doubloons. The historian Voldigan, in his history of the reign of the Emperor Adovian, mentions something called a doblon, which was then worth two oxen, four sheep or six pigs. The poet Persimmian, in his epic, *The Persimmianade,* does mention the doubloon, which was worth one male slave, one and a half female slaves or ..."

"Or what, Civil Servant 21346?"

"Two occasions in a first-class brothel, Lord High Admiral."

The Admiral allowed himself to be shocked.

"I am shocked, Civil Servant 21346, shocked. Is the poet Persimmian on any educational curriculum?"

"I believe *The Persimmianade* is taught in all Orson schools, Lord High Admiral. It is much admired in literary circles."

If there was one thing the Admiral detested more than insolent civil servants, it was literary types.

"Have all the works of Persimmian removed from the school curriculum immediately. We can't have that sort of filth poisoning the minds of our young."

"Yes, Lord High Admiral."

The Admiral leaned back, congratulating himself on his decisiveness, then remembered the business at hand.

"Doubloons, Civil Servant 21346. Have you decided what a doubloon is worth?"

Civil Servant 21346 hesitated, but decided he had no option but to bite the bullet.

"Taking everything into account, Lord High Admiral, I can only give an approximate estimate, which is that a gold doubloon would be worth between one hundred and twenty and one hundred and fifty Galactic Units of Account."

It took him a few moments to do the calculation, but this time the Admiral really was shocked.

"Are you saying that Sloakum might be asking for more than two million?"

Civil Servant 21346 hesitated again.

"A little less, Lord High Admiral."

"Not much less, Civil Servant 21346. That's a great deal of money. Have we collected that much gold?"

"Not yet, Lord High Admiral."

"Will we collect that much, Civil Servant 21346?"

"Possibly not, Lord High Admiral."

"Possibly not, Civil Servant 21346?"

"Probably not, Lord High Admiral."

"*Probably* not, Civil Servant 21346?"

"Er, not, Lord High Admiral."

"Why not, Civil Servant 21346?"

Inwardly, Civil Servant 21346 oscillated between apprehension and exultation.

"Because, Lord High Admiral, there does not appear to be that much gold on Orson, unless …"

"Unless what, Civil Servant 21346?"

"Unless we include all the gold jewellery on Orson."

The Admiral's stock response to any unwelcome fact was to deny it and make sure he knew who to blame if it turned out to be true.

"Nonsense, Civil Servant 21346. Go and find it. In the meantime we may need what you have collected for Sloakum to pay this ransom."

Civil Servant 21346 slunk out of the office. As he watched him go, the Admiral felt the sense of panic that had been eating at him for some time beginning to mount.

13

When they returned to the kitchen, Nimbolt handed Junipa a knife and told her to slice some vegetables.

"Look as if you are working, or else one of the Qwezellarans will start asking questions about you."

Junipa had not prepared food since she was very young. There were limits to Feminarch egalitarianism. She began to slice clumsily, but, after a couple of minutes, the knife slipped and cut her finger. She gave a slight gasp and put her finger to her mouth. Nimbolt saw what had happened and took her into a small room next to the kitchen, where he opened a cupboard. He took out a small device and put it on her finger. The bleeding stopped. She decided they needed to talk further.

"Nimbolt, when I talked to the slave girls they told me about some persons being held captive here. I think I know who one of them is, and I need to talk to him. Do you know where he might be?"

Junipa could see that Nimbolt was not sure that he could entirely trust her. She had to take him into her confidence.

"Nimbolt, I want to tell you something about me. Can I trust you to keep it secret?"

Again he hesitated, but then nodded. She decided to take the risk.

"I am also female."

He stared at her, wide-eyed.

"How did you get here?"

"I can't tell you that, but it is important – more important than you could imagine – that I speak to those captives. Do you know where they are?"

Again he hesitated, but this time replied.

"I heard from another slave, Denfrith, that there were strangers in the guest apartments. That might be them."

"Did this Denfrith say anything about them?"

"No, but he did say that they were strangers, not Qwezellarans."

"Is that unusual?"

"Yes. Those apartments are for members of the Qwezellaran priesthood."

"That must be them. So are they really captives or just guests?"

He shrugged.

"I don't know."

"Guests or not, I need to speak to one of them. How do I get to these apartments?"

Nimbolt had to think.

"Denfrith serves the apartments. I am friendly with him and he is also lazy and loves to play games. If I offer to take on his duties for an hour or two, I am sure he will agree."

"Good plan, Nimbolt. You can take me with you."

He looked at her sternly.

"We must be very careful. You must say nothing until I say so."

Nimbolt went off to find Denfrith. He came back several minutes later.

"Denfrith has agreed. He was due to take them food in half an hour, so we will go instead."

Junipa smiled in gratitude and then a thought occurred to her.

"Nimbolt, are there any listening devices in those rooms?"

Nimbolt shook his head.

"Such things are not allowed here."

Junipa followed Nimbolt as they passed through two long corridors before they arrived at the guest apartments. Outside the door, there was a figure asleep in a chair. He awoke briefly and looked at them as they entered, before nodding off again.

They had come into a large room, its walls painted in a light cream colour. Two settees were arranged round a table and on them she saw the figures of de la Beche and Doctor Culpepper. As Junipa looked around she saw Jim sitting in a chair by the window, staring out. They appeared to be alone. She and Nimbolt put the food down on the table.

"Cream tea," said Doctor Culpepper, gazing with some pleasure at the scones, cakes and cream laid out before them. "At least we can't complain about the food, Sechy."

De la Beche had been fiddling with his communicator, before tossing it aside.

"Culinary matters are the least of our problems, Sawbones. That thing is still dead. Nothing works here. These people seem to have a fetish for the primitive."

Junipa saw her opportunity. She looked at Nimbolt to see if it was safe to speak. He gave a small nod.

"Captain de la Beche," she said softly.

De la Beche responded wearily.

"Yes?"

"You do not know me, but I know of you. My name is Junipa Penthiliopesdotter. I have been sent here by Her Feminence, Orestia Penthiliopesdotter, whom I believe you do know."

Jim had been watching the newcomers, and saw a look of surprise flash briefly across the Captain's face as Junipa spoke.

"Well, this is a surprise," said de la Beche. "Do give my compliments to Her Feminence when you next see her. I wish I could say it was also pleasure, but I assume you, too, are an involuntary guest of our hosts, the Qwezallarans – or am I to assume you are in cahoots with them?"

"Neither," replied Junipa. "I'm here to help you, if I can."

De la Beche gave a wry smile.

"I don't want to sound ungrateful, but what could you do to help? Besides, what interest do you and Her Feminence have in anything that happens to us?"

Junipa decided it was best to be frank.

"We wouldn't normally be interested in the absurd antics of a bunch of unreconstructed males. However, we know that the Orsonians want to use you as a pawn in their Galactic games. They've hired the appalling pirate Sloakum to capture you. And, if that happens, we Feminarchs could be in mortal danger. My mission is to prevent you falling into the hands of the Orsonians."

De la Beche gave another half smile.

"That's all very well, but how do you think you might accomplish this 'mission' of yours? Do you imagine you could simply lead us out of this place without anyone noticing?"

Junipa had to acknowledge that there was something of a gap between mission and plan.

"I admit it won't be easy. How about your crew? Could I contact them and tell them where you are?"

"You could, but I doubt that they would be able to do anything. You may have noticed that only the most primitive weapons technologies work here. My lot can handle swords, axes and cudgels and I'm sure they could give a good account of themselves, but there are far too many down here for them to overcome. Besides, we would need to be quick. I imagine that the Qwezallarans are even now haggling with Sloakum and another bunch about the ransom."

"Do you have any other suggestions as to how we might be able to get you out of here?"

De la Beche grimaced.

"Only one that Sawbones here has come up with and it's, how do I put it, tricky."

"Tricky?"

"It is, a bit," said Culpepper. He took a small device from his out of tunic. "I could use this to put Sechy in a sort of coma, so that he appears to be dead from a stroke. Then the Qwezallarans would have to let him go."

Junipa was intrigued.

"What is that thing and what's tricky about it?"

It was Culpepper's turn to grimace.

"It's a very useful little tool. Does lots of things a Doctor like me needs to do. The problem is that I've never actually used it to induce a stroke before and the settings are a bit ...",

"Tricky?" asked Junipa.

"Tricky," agreed Culpepper. "If I get them wrong he could actually be dead, instead of just seeming to be."

It was then that an idea occurred to Jim.

"What about the Knights?"

De la Beche and Doctor Culpepper both turned towards Jim, while Junipa looked on bemused.

"It's a thought, Sechy," said Doctor Culpepper. "They are certainly the boys to give anyone a whacking."

"What are you talking about?" said Junipa.

"The Knights of the Sacred Circle," said Jim. "They dress in suits of armour and ride their fiery steeds and do deeds."

That sounded like typical male nonsense to Junipa, but was there an alternative?

"Are you saying that these Knights might rescue you?"

"I think they might," said Culpepper. "After all, Sechy is *Sir* Sechaverall de la Beche, a fellow Knight. Chivalry demands no less."

"And he has sat in the Siege Perilous," added Jim.

"Absolutely," agreed Culpepper. "That means he is the Chosen One. They are duty bound to come to his aid."

Junipa was now convinced that this *was* typical male nonsense, but felt she had no option but to go along with it.

"How do I contact these Knights?"

"I assume you are able to leave the Grand Kalaba," said de la Beche.

"I hope so."

"Then you must find the Bonhumes. They have a little priory somewhere near here. Ask for Bon August and tell him you are from me and need to contact the Knights. He can summon them. When they come, the person you need to speak to is Squire Squire."

"Squire Squire?"

"Yes, well it makes sense they way he tells it. Squire Squire is a smart young fellow. Tell him everything you can, and let's see what he can come up with – and tell him to be quick."

Junipa took out her communicator.

"I will need some proof that I've seen you. This thing can still record. It's about the only thing it's good for here. Give this Squire Squire a message."

De la Beche smiled and looked straight at the communicator.

"Greetings, Squire Squire. I'm afraid that my companions and I are in a bit of a pickle. The Great Sandjanum has decided to lock us up while he sells us to a notorious pirate. We're trying to find a way out, but right at the moment, things don't look too hopeful. Anything you and my fellow Knights can do would be much appreciated."

14

The Bonhumes' priory appeared out of the mist. Junipa had trudged for hours to find it. No cabs had been available and, even if there had been, they would not have got near. There was no road, only a narrow path. She would never have found it but for directions from a couple of kindly monks who had been planting crops in a field along the way.

There appeared to be no one about. No lights could be seen in the windows. She approached the large wooden door and knocked on it with her fist as loudly as she could. The door remained closed, so she knocked again. Eventually it was opened by a fresh-faced figure in a long brown robe.

"I wish to speak to Bon August," said Junipa.

The figure nodded and gestured for her to enter. She was led into a white-walled room with a large wooden table and invited to sit. He left. Several minutes later, another robed figure, this time with bald pate and a long, flowing beard, appeared.

"I am Bon August. You wish to speak with me?"

She decided that she needed to come to the point straightaway.

"I have come from Captain de la Beche. You know of him?"

Bon August nodded.

"Yes, of course, Captain de la Beche. He came here. Are you a pilgrim also?"

"Pardon?"

"Are you a pilgrim, seeking enlightenment, like Captain de la Beche?"

Junipa was unsure of what he was saying, but decided to go along with it.

"In a way. I am seeking the Knights of the Sacred Circle. I believe you know them?"

Bon August looked doubtful.

"Yes, I know of them, but I am not sure they aid pilgrims. Their's is a different calling."

"So I understand. That's why I need to find them. Captain de la Beche is being held against his will by the Qwezellarans. They intend to ransom him to a pirate, a monstrous villain. I am hoping that the Knights can help him."

Bon August took a few moments to ingest this news.

"Captain de la Beche a prisoner – and for a ransom, you say? That is most troubling. Perhaps the Knights can help. Their sacred mission is to right wrongs – and to find Grails."

Junipa thought she would leave Grail-hunting aside for the moment.

"Exactly. This is a wrong that needs to be put right. How do we find the Knights?"

Bon August pointed a finger upwards.

"We will fly their banner from the tower. They will come."

* * *

A light rain was falling as Junipa saw the mounted figures appear out of the mist. She gazed in astonishment at the ironclad Knights, their armour streaked with rust, as the donkeys, wet and bedraggled, trudged forward. They drew up to the priory and halted. Junipa gathered herself to speak.

"My name is Junipa Penthiliopesdotter. Is one of you Squire Squire?"

Another figure, this time dressed in hose and doublet, came forward.

"That's me, squire. Squire Squire at your service. What can I do for you, Squire?"

Junipa wasn't quite sure she followed.

"Excuse me. Who is squire here?"

Squire Squire grinned.

"I'm Squire Squire, and I call you Squire. That way we're all squire, if you see what I mean?"

Junipa didn't see, but decided to ignore it and come straight to the point.

"I have come from Captain de la Beche, who I believe you know. He is being held prisoner by the Qwezellarans in their Grand Kalaba. They intend to ransom him to a pirate by the name of Sloakum and you can imagine what his fate would be. He is hoping you might help him."

Squire Squire sucked in his cheeks.

"That sounds nasty, very nasty indeed, but rescuing isn't in our contract."

Junipa shook her head in disbelief.

"What do you mean, contract?"

"We've got a Grail-finding contract with him. Nothing in it about rescues."

She took a few seconds to realize what he was talking about.

"Is this contract about the Kwokkah?"

"Yes."

"Have you found it?"

"Not yet."

"Do you know where it is?"

"Not exactly."

"You mean you have no idea where it is?"

"I suppose you could put it like that."

Junipa shook her head again.

"It seems to me, Squire Squire, that you're falling down on your side of the contract."

Squire Squire frowned.

"Look, let me be straight with you. I don't know who you are. You come here with this story about Sir Sechaverell. How do I know you are telling the truth? We get a lot of tale-tellers around here, and your one sounds a pretty tall tale indeed. You might be making it all up for some evil purpose."

Junipa's voice rose.

"What possible 'evil purpose' would I have for concocting such a story? How would I know about de la Beche?"

She took out her communicator and showed him de la Beche's message.

"Convinced now?"

Squire Squire was not entirely convinced.

"It's him, I'll give you that, but he could have been forced to say it."

Junipa stamped her foot in exasperation.

"Do you think de la Beche could be forced to say anything like that? I thought Knights believed in chivalry. Isn't *Sir* Secheverell de la Beche one of you? What's more, I understand he is the Chosen One, because he sat in the Siege something or other. How would I know that if I hadn't seen him?"

Squire Squire had to acknowledge that she had a point.

"Technically, you have a point."

"Technically?"

"Well, all right, you have a point, but rescues don't come cheap. Chivalry is all very well, but you can't do it on a pittance. The Knights have got overheads – castles, tournaments, all that stuff."

Junipa was not impressed.

"Chivalry is all very well, is it? What exactly is chivalrous about something, if you have to pay for it every time?"

Squire Squire's expression took on a look of injured innocence.

"We offer a top of the range chivalric service – daring deeds, righting wrongs, finding Grails, rescuing damsels in distress, the lot. You won't find finer anywhere. And we do *pro bono* work for good causes."

Hearing his protestations, Junipa suddenly saw an opening.

"Have they ever rescued a damsel in distress?"

Squire Squire shrugged.

"Not as such. There aren't any damsels on Utrophia."

"What if I told you there *were*? Would you be willing to rescue them?"

Junipa saw Squire Squire's eyes widen in astonishment.

"Them? You mean there are more than one?"

"There are twelve."

Squire Squire's eyes narrowed.

"Are you sure? Where are they, and how could they have got here?"

"I'm absolutely sure. I have met them. They are in the Grand Kalaba as well. The Qwezellarans have made them slaves and they claim that slaves are chattels, not persons, so can be brought to Utrophia legitimately. Not what you would call chivalrous behaviour, is it?"

Squire Squire looked at her as if he could hardly believe what he was hearing.

"Why should I believe you?"

Junipa decided she had to play her last card.

"Because I am female, too. Do you want me to prove it?"

She lifted her hand to draw back her tunic. For just an instant, Squire Squire froze as he caught a glimpse of flesh.

"No, I believe you now. We would be honoured to rescue them – *pro bono*, of course," he added hastily.

"Together with de la Beche and his companions?"

Squire Squire saw he had no option.

"Naturally. We don't do things by halves."

He turned to face the Knights.

"Gentil Knights, be ye of passing good cheer for ye have vowed this day to seek deliveraunce from dolorous prisonment at the hands of knavish Qwezellarans of a passing douzaine of demosels and of the gentil knight, Sir Sechaverell de la Beche and his retainers. Beseemeth ye that that all is meet and good?"

A roar of approval went up from the Knights as they waved swords and lances in the air.

15

Junipa was adamant.

"I don't think charging into the Grand Kalaba is a good idea."

Squire Squire shrugged.

"Personally, I agree with you, but the Knights like a good charge. Besides, the idea of rescuing damsels in distress has gone to their heads. It's made them very frisky."

Junipa shook her head in exasperation. What was it about the male psyche that seemed to short-circuit reason, whenever sex was concerned? She was more than ever convinced that, in any rational society, males would be redundant.

"For pity's sake, tell them to calm down. From what I have seen, the place is a fortress. There are armed guards everywhere. What would they do if they got, in except create mayhem and hope somehow to rescue the hostages? Most likely they would be cut down by the guards. We need a plan to get in and out of the Grand Kalaba before the Qwezellarans realize what is happening."

Squire Squire shrugged again.

"Easier said than done. What do you have in mind?"

Junipa had to acknowledge that she had only a vague idea of a plan, but she had to start somewhere.

"First, we need to get de la Beche and the female slaves together in one place. Then, we need to find a way to get the Knights in before the alarm can be raised."

Squire Squire looked at her sceptically.

"You call that a plan?"

"No, it's not a plan, but it is a start. There is another way into the Grand Kalaba. It's round the back and it's where they deliver the goods. It seems to be only lightly guarded. I've been in there myself and I know someone inside who I think might help us. We go in, get the hostages together and then call in the Knights to get us out."

Squire Squire nodded.

"As you say, it's a start, but there are a lot of gaps. How do you propose to get all the hostages together?"

"I accept that it will be tricky. We'll have to work it out once we get inside. One thing I need to stress is that the Knights have to keep out of sight until the last minute, otherwise the Qwezellarans might become suspicious. How do you propose calling them? I don't suppose they have anything like a communicator?"

Squire Squire shook his head.

"Knights don't do that sort of thing. I'll use a bugle."

"A what?"

He reached into a pouch by his side and pulled out what Junipa saw was a small, brass, flared tube. He blew into it and it emitted what sounded like a series of caterwauls.

"That's a bugle. I play the right call and they will come."

It was Junipa's turn to be sceptical, but she knew she had no better idea.

"We're agreed on the start. The first thing you and I need to do is to get into the Grand Kalaba. After that, we're going to have to play it by ear."

***

Junipa took Squire Squire to the rear of the Grand Kalaba. In front of the gates stood a uniformed sentry holding a large battle axe. She hesitated, unsure of what to do next. Squire Squire continued to walk forward.

"He'll stop us if we try to get in," said Junipa.

"That's what we want," replied Squire Squire.

"What?"

"Trust me," came the reply.

Squire Squire walked up to the sentry, who thrust out the battle axe and shouted "Halt."

"At ease, squire," said Squire Squire, looking him up and down. "I can see you are a smart young fellow who likes to think about his future."

The sentry stared back at him without speaking, a look of puzzlement spreading over his face.

"Now, can I ask," continued Squire Squire, "have you made sure your nearest and dearest are taken care of if anything should happen to you? Built up a little nest egg? Put anything by for a rainy day?"

The sentry remained silent, but was now completely puzzled.

"The reason I ask is that it is important with these things to start young. I take it that you are here on service from your home planet. Can I ask if you are married?"

Surprise replaced puzzlement in the sentry's expression. He blurted out an answer.

"No."

"Very wise. No need to take on such a responsibility so young. Who is your next of kin? Your father?"

"My mother."

"Ah, your mother," said Squire Squire, smiling sympathetically. "Widowed is she?"

The sentry nodded.

"So she has only her little boy to rely on. If anything happened to you, she'd be in a pickle, wouldn't she?"

The sentry nodded again and Junipa thought she saw his eyes moistening.

"Worry not," said Squire Squire. "This could be your lucky day. I think I can help you. Can I ask your name?"

The sentry looked from one to the other and swallowed before answering.

"Javana Sipahi."

"Well, Javana, if I may call you that, allow me to introduce myself. My name is Squire Squire and I represent the Everlasting Life Corporation. You must have heard of them. We are the largest insurance company in the Galaxy."

Javana's expression told Junipa that he was not well acquainted with the Everlasting Life Corporation.

"We have policies to suit all needs," continued Squire Squire, "and the one I have especially in mind for you is our 'Save Safe and Prosper' full-benefits package. You put in a small sum every month and you get all the benefits from day one. If you get injured, say you lose a leg or a hand, we pay out, no questions asked. If the worst came to the worst and you passed away before full term, your mother would get enough to keep her in comfort for the rest of her days. And, best of all, at the end of the term, you have a nice little nest egg that you can put towards buying the home of your dreams. What could be better?"

Junipa could see from his expression that he was attracted to the idea, but worried that perhaps he should not be.

"You said I would have to put in a small sum every month. How much?"

"I can see you are a smart young fellow, Javana. That's the question you need to ask, but let me reassure you. We always customize a package to suit the client's financial circumstances. However, I can go further. Today is the start of our special promotion, a promotion designed especially for someone like you, just starting out in business. Sign up today and you get the first year free. All the benefits from day one and nothing to pay for a year. How does that sound to you?"

Junipa could see his interest was rising, but he didn't want to seem too eager.

"Well, I suppose it doesn't sound too bad."

"Not too bad, Javana?" said Squire Squire, injecting a note of incredulity into his voice. "Not too bad? I can see you're a difficult fellow to please, but I think I can add a little something that will convince you. You are not the only one who could benefit from all that Everlasting Life has to offer. I'm sure that you would like all your colleagues inside the Grand Kalaba to have the opportunity. If you allow me in to talk to them then, if I am as good as I think I am – and I am – I'll have them all signed up in no time. You would of course receive an introducer fee for each one, because you would, in effect, be introducing them to me. I'm sure that would more than cover the premiums for your Save Safe and Prosper policy. Think about it, Javana. This is the opportunity of a lifetime. You would have secured your financial future entirely for free. How good is that?"

Javana stared at him. He seemed struck almost dumb with gratitude and could only mumble a thank you. Squire Squire took a small device from his pouch and began to enter details. He looked up after a few seconds.

"All done. I'll bring the policy for you to sign once we know the amount of your introducers' fees. If you could let us in, we can get to work for you."

Javana pulled a lever and the gates swung open. They walked towards the kitchen of the Grand Kalaba.

"Nicely done," said Junipa in a low voice. "I almost believed you."

"You should," replied Squire Squire.

"What do you mean?"

"I *do* represent the Everlasting Life Corporation."

"What?"

"You don't think the Knights pay me enough, do you? They're a stingy lot. I need to earn a bit on the side."

Junipa could only shake her head. Was there no end to male deviousness?

16

Commander Splenditheran listened to his Chief of Staff in complete disbelief.

"What do you mean, they are going to declare independence?"

"I told you the Nullarboreans were full of shit."

Splenditheran resolved to send the Chief of Staff on a course in verbal communication, but now was not the time.

"I don't want your opinion. I want to know exactly what they are saying."

The Chief of Staff considered "full of shit" an adequate description of almost any situation, but, if Splenditheran wanted it spelt out, he would give it to him.

"They said they are leaving the Confederation and setting up as an independent planet. They don't want all their rules and regulations to be set by outsiders and they want to sign treaties with all the other organizations in the Galaxy."

Splenditheran thought that was outrageous.

"That's outrageous. Tell them that, if they leave, we will invade."

"They say that if we try to invade, they will defect to the Orsonians and take other planets with them."

Splenditheran glared at the Chief of Staff for several seconds before replying.

"Well, you had better think of something else to be done – and be quick about it."

The Chief of Staff knew exactly what was to be done. Splenditheran was full of shit and it was only a matter of time before he took over.

The Lord High Admiral of the Orsonian Battle Fleet listened to Civil Servant 21346 in complete disbelief.

"What do you mean, they are going to declare independence?"

Civil Servant 21346 had the familiar task of having to tell the Admiral a thing more than once before he grasped it.

"The Nullarboreans said they are leaving the Confederation and setting up as an independent planet. They don't want all their rules and regulations to be set by outsiders and they want to sign treaties with all the other organizations in the Galaxy."

The Admiral thought that was outrageous.

"That's outrageous. Tell them, the moment they do, we will invade."

"They say that if we try to invade, they will go back to the Southern Cross Federation and take several other of our planets with them."

The Admiral glared at Civil Servant 21346 for several seconds before replying.

"Well you had better prepare a plan of something else to be done – and be quick about it."

Civil Servant 21346 knew exactly what he had to do. He said to himself, "Organize and they will come."

Orestia listened to Sahaika in complete disbelief.

"What do you mean, they are going to declare independence?"

Sahaika was Junipa's assistant, taking her place while she was on Utrophia. She was bright, effervescent and utterly intimidated by Orestia.

"The Nullarboreans said they are leaving the Confederation and setting up as an independent planet, Your Feminence. They don't want all their rules and regulations to be set by outsiders and they want to sign treaties with all the other organizations in the Galaxy."

Orestia thought that was the best news that she had heard for a long time.

"That's the best news that I've heard for a long time, though I doubt that the Orsonians and the Southern Cross would agree. I bet they are outraged, but what can they do? If either of them try to invade, it would only make things worse for themselves. They'll be at daggers drawn, each keeping their eye on the other, so they won't bother about us. It's perfect."

Sahaika thought she understood, although she knew little about high politics.

"What about Junipa, Your Feminence?"

Orestia felt a frisson of horror. The Kwokkah! What if de la Beche found it and gave it to the Southern Cross Federation? That could make the Nullaboreans change their minds.

"Contact Junipa. Tell her to get back to Utrophia and make sure that de la Beche does not get his hands on the Kwokkah. Give him to Sloakum, if she has to."

Sahaika trembled, but knew she had to answer.

"I'm afraid I am not able to do that, Your Feminence."

"Why ever not?"

"Because communication with Utrophia is only allowed to religious organizations."

17

Junipa looked around the kitchen and saw Nimbolt tending to a pan on a large stove. She took Squire Squire by the arm and went over to him.

"Nimbolt," she whispered, "I want you to meet someone who's going to help you get out of here. Is there somewhere we can talk?"

Nimbolt indicated a door leading to a large pantry. They went in.

"The name's Squire Squire," said Squire Squire. "Pleased to meet you, Squire."

Nimbolt stared back, not sure what to reply.

"He calls everyone squire," explained Junipa.

"Even you, Gruff?" asked Nimbolt.

"Gruff?" said Squire Squire. "I thought you said your name was … "

"Never mind," interrupted Junipa, "Let's get down to business. We need to find a way of getting de la Beche and the dancers out of here. Squire Squire has arranged a rescue, but we need to make sure we know where they are and preferably get them all in one place."

"What do you mean, 'arranged a rescue'?" asked a clearly doubtful Nimbolt.

"The Knights of the Sacred Circle," replied Squire Squire.

"The Knights of the Sacred Circle?" said an even more sceptical Nimbolt. "Why would they want to rescue us?"

"Rescuing damsels in distress is what they do," said Squire Squire. "You will see them when they come, mounted on their fiery steeds."

"They have said they will come," said Junipa. "That much I can confirm, but we need to decide what we do first."

"Am I right," asked Squire Squire, "that we know where they all are, but they are well guarded?"

"Yes," said Nimbolt.

"In that case, my strategy is always to go to the top. Who's the Big Cheese around here?"

"Pardon?" said Nimbolt.

"Who calls the shots? Who's in charge?"

"I suppose that would be the Great Sandjanum."

"Right, take me to him."

"I can't do that," said Nimbolt, a note of fear creeping into his voice. "He lives in his own suite. There are guards. You wouldn't be allowed in."

"Oh, wouldn't I?" said Squire Squire. "Where is this suite?"

Nimbolt shook his head, but acceded.

"Go out of the kitchen, through the lobby, then up the staircase into the hall. At the other end, you will see a set of big doors with sentries either side. That's the entry to the suite of the Great Sandjanum."

Squire Squire turned to Junipa.

"I need you to come with me."

Junipa was taken aback.

"Why?"

"It looks more official. You're going to be the Chief Risk Assessor and Actuary for the Everlasting Life Corporation."

"What! I haven't the faintest idea what you're talking about."

"You don't need to. All you need to do is look stern and nod or shake your head when I say something. Got it?"

Junipa shook her head and looked stern.

"No."

"That's the ticket," said Squire Squire. "Let's go."

They went out of the kitchen and up a grand marble staircase that swept up to a large vaulted hall with a painted ceiling and statues occupying numerous alcoves. At one end they could see two large gilded doors guarded by sentries wearing elaborate uniforms and high, plumed hats. They marched quickly up to the door.

"We've come to see the Great Sandjanum," announced Squire Squire.

A flicker of derision crossed the sentries' face.

"Oh, have you?" said one. "Do you by any chance have an appointment?"

Squire Squire glared at the sentry for several seconds before answering.

"We are from the Everlasting Life Corporation and we are here to do the annual inspection of premises to ensure that all its insurance policies are up to date. These are urgent matters and I have no doubt that Great Sandjanum will wish to see us."

Derision was replaced by uncertainty in the sentries' expression. They looked at one another and then one pushed a button by the side of the door.

"Wait here."

After a short interval, a figure dressed in white robe and turban arrived. He regarded them suspiciously.

"You are wishing to be seeing the Great Sandjanum?"

"Yes," replied Squire Squire. "As I have already explained, we represent the Everlasting Life Corporation and were are here to conduct the annual review of your organization's insurance policies."

The turbaned figure seemed bemused.

"By what are you meaning, 'insurance policies'?"

"These are confidential financial matters," said Squire Squire sternly. "They are of great importance and I am only authorized to discuss them with the head of your organization, who I understand to be the Great Sandjanum. Is that correct?"

"He is being the Great Sandjanum, to whom we are all deferring in all matters."

"Exactly, so take me to him now please. Neither of us will be wanting to waste time."

The turbaned figure hesitated for a few seconds before speaking.

"Please be coming with me."

They walked through the doors and into a long hall decorated with paintings, both portraits and what Junipa took to be religious scenes. Eventually, they came to another set of gilded doors, guarded by another beplumed sentry. The turbaned figure waved a hand; the sentry opened the doors.

They entered a large, domed, lavishly-decorated room. Around its sides were tables, behind which more turbaned figures were seated. At the other end of the room they saw a portly, bearded figure sitting on a throne.

"Your Great Sandjanimity, this is being the reviewers of insurance," announced their guide as they approached.

The Great Sandjanum glowered at them.

"What is this insurance nonsense?"

"Allow me to introduce ourselves," said Squire Squire. "I represent the Everlasting Life Corporation and this is our Chief Risk Assessor and Actuary. We are your insurance agents. We cover you for all risks. You pay just a little bit each year and, if anything bad happens to you or yours, we pay out so that you can keep the whole show on the road, so to speak. Now, in order to do that, we need to make sure all your policies are up to date. That's why we are here."

Junipa thought the Great Sandjanum was about to explode. He glared at them with the combination of contempt and distaste that he normally reserved for the deepest-dyed idolator.

"I have never heard of nonsense like insurance."

"Ah, yes. You wouldn't have," replied Squire Squire. "That's because the policy has changed. It's the new policy now."

"What is this new policy?"

"It's different from the old policy."

The Great Sandjanum struggled to control his exasperation.

"And what was the old policy?"

"The old policy," replied Squire Squire, "was that all the business was handled by head office back on your home planet, so that you weren't bothered with the admin. But, between you and me, Everlasting Life had their fingers burned when some organizations spotted loopholes and started claiming for things that never happened or weren't covered. They sued and you know what the law's like – a lottery. So now, Everlasting Life has a new policy. Everything has to be inspected on site to make sure there aren't any loopholes."

The Great Sandjanum was losing the struggle with his exasperation.

"We have no need of trifles like insurance. We rely on the benevolence of the all-knowing, all-powerful Qudai. All blessings to Him."

Squire Squire nodded.

"*You* may do, and all credit to you. Qudai takes care of all your spiritual needs, but," he added, gesturing, "what about all this?"

The Great Sandjanum stared at him in surprise.

"All this? Are you talking about the Grand Kalaba?"

"Exactly. Very nice Grand Kalaba you've got here. Wouldn't want anything nasty to happen to it."

The Great Sandjanum's eyes narrowed. He thought he detected a threat.

"The Grand Kalaba has been here through ages and nothing has happened to it."

"So you say, but what if it fell down or you had a fire? You never know what might happen. I'll need to see your Building Integrity Report and your Fire Safety Certificate."

The Great Sandjanum shook his head in disbelief.

"Fire? Fire? The only fire we dread is the all-consuming fire of the abode of the damned, ruled over by the devil Ekwensu."

"I don't have any devil's abodes on my list for inspection," replied Squire Squire, "but Everlasting Life covers everyone, so I expect our rep there will want to see his Fire Safety Certificate too. Are you saying you don't have one?"

The face of the Great Sandjanum turned scarlet.

"I pronounce anathema on all Fire Safety Certificates! All who possess them are heretics and infidels!"

There was a sharp intake of breath by Squire Squire.

"No certificate, eh? Your premiums are going to go through the roof without a certificate."

He looked to Junipa, who shook her head sternly.

"And I don't even want to think about the excess you would have to pay on any claim. We probably wouldn't even be able to take you on."

Junipa nodded even more sternly in agreement as Squire Squire continued.

"Let me tell you what could happen if you don't have proper insurance. You've heard of the Indushetians?"

The Great Sandjanum had a dim memory of infidels from an obscure planet.

"Yes."

"Well, their Grand Temple caught fire and burnt down. Not a brick left standing. Their Big Cheese, who called himself the Annointed One and had more titles than you could count, had forgotten to renew the insurance. When his people found out they were mad. He got done for everything from grand larceny to apostasy."

The Great Sandjanum shuddered.

"Apostasy?"

"Yes, apostasy. Failure in his sacred duty to protect the temple meant he was trusting to the false god of luck. They don't take apostasy lightly, don't the Indushetians. Being torn limb from limb was the least of his worries."

He looked again to Junipa, who shook her head sternly and sadly.

"Now, I'm not saying there's going to be a big fire or anything like that here," continued Squire Squire, "but we can't afford to take chances, can we? What would your head office say if you had an earthquake or a fire?"

The Great Sandjanum appeared to be taken aback.

"What do you mean, head office?"

"The ones that sent you here."

The Great Sandjanum drew himself up on his throne.

"I was sent here by His Most Serene Sublimity, the Supreme Hierophactor of Qwezellar, to testify to the word of Qudai on Utrophia."

"Of course you were," said Squire Squire, "but what would you testify to His Most Serene Sublimity if the Grand Kalaba burnt down and there was no insurance money to rebuild it?"

The Great Sandjanum shuddered inwardly. The holy rages of His Most Serene Sublimity inspired fear and awe in all who beheld them. All-consuming fire and the tender mercies of the devil Ekwensu would almost be preferable. He decided that a little discretion might be in order.

"How might I obtain such a certificate?"

Squire Squire pursed his lips.

"Well, first you need to find a Fire Safety Inspector. There are not many of them round here."

The Great Sandjanum did not doubt it.

"Do you know of one?"

"As it happens, I do. As a matter of fact, I am a fully-qualified Fire Safety Inspector."

"So you could give me a certificate?"

Squire Squire pursed his lips again.

"It's a bit irregular. I'm supposed to be inspecting your policies, not handing out certificates." He paused, considering the options. "However, as it's you, I'll make an exception. There will be a cost though."

The Great Sandjanum did not doubt thateither.

"How much would you ask?"

"Oh, we're not talking about money. Not where safety is concerned," came the reply.

The Great Sandjanum was relieved to hear it.

"However," continued Squire Squire, "there is something that you can sort out for me. Wearing my other hat, I am Squire to the Knights of the Sacred Circle. You know of them, of course?"

The Great Sandjanum certainly did know of them. They were second only to His Most Serene Sublimity in their ability to strike fear and awe.

"Now, a little dickie bird tells me that you have one of their number here: Sir Sechaverell de la Beche."

The Great Sandjanum was astonished. He had no idea that de la Beche was a knight.

"*Sir* Sechaverell, is it? I had no idea. You are correct. Captain de la Beche is a guest here."

"From what the dickie bird told me, guest isn't quite the right word, is it? It said you were planning to sell him to the Sempiternal Ecclesia."

The Great Sandjanum struggled mightily to hide both surprise and anger. He silently called down the wrath of Qudai on all dickie birds.

"That is a gross calumny. We would never do such a thing as sell him. The Sempiternal Ecclesia informed us that Captain de la Beche had committed some particularly heinous offences against their beliefs – idolatrous as they undoubtedly are – and in a fraternal spirit, we agreed to hand him over to them, so that they could subject him to a due process of enquiry."

"I believe you, of course," said Squire Squire. "I like to take everyone at their word, but the Knights are a bit less trusting. Deeds are what Knights trust, not words. They are outside, threatening to break in and rescue Sir Sechaverell. It was all I could do to hold them back."

"That would be outrageous, a sacrilege."

Squire Squire nodded sympathetically.

"It would. I'm with you there. I'm on your side, but it can be hard to hold back a Knight in armour on his fiery steed when his dander is up. There's no arguing with them sometimes."

The Great Sandjanum stared at Squire Squire, weighing up whether to believe him or not. He decided that the possible consequences of not believing him were worse than believing.

"What are you suggesting?"

"Well," said Squire Squire, "I think we can do a deal here. You need a certificate. I'll give you one and I'll go one better. I'll take all the admin off your hands and send it back to head office with a promise that the premiums will be no higher than last year. They'll lap it up. For your part, you will invite the Knights in, hand Sir Sechaverell over to them and then we'll all be friends. How does that sound?"

The Great Sandjanum wasn't sure it sounded particularly good but it was at least better than any other option he could think of at that moment. Handing de la Beche over meant no more gold, but the propect of a wrecked Grand Kalaba and the wrath of His Most Serene Sublimity was much worse.

"Agreed."

"Excellent," said Squire Squire. "Now I know you'll want to make it up to Sir Sechaverell for all the inconvenience you've caused, so how about throwing a little party for him. I hear you do celebrations very nicely here, with singing and dancing."

The Great Sandjanum decided he had to make the best of it.

"Naturally, I would not like Sir Sechaverell to think badly of us." He clapped his hands and a turban approached. "Bring Captain de la Beche and his companions here."

"I will go and summon the Knights," said Squire Squire. "I'll bring them in by the rear gates. Less fuss that way."

The Great Sandjanum waved assent and watched as Squire Squire and Junipa left the grand hall. They made their way through the kitchen, neither saying anything until they were out into the courtyard. Finally, Junipa was able to voice her anxieties.

"Are you sure this is going to work?"

"It's worked so far."

"What do we do if it doesn't?"

"How fast can you run?"

Junipa could think of nothing to say.

As they approached the gate, Squire Squire gave a thumbs up.

"Going good, Javana. The Great Sandjanum's signed up. Your fortune's made. Open up for me, will you?"

Javana beamed and opened the gates. Squire Squire took the bugle out of his pouch and blew a series of notes. In less than a minute, Junipa heard the clopping of hooves on stone and along the road there appeared the Knights on their donkeys. Squire Squire acknowledged each one, as they were led in by Sir Agravain.

"Sir Brunor, Sir Cador, Sir Dagonet, Sir Esclabor, Sir Gaheris, Sir Galeschin, Sir Hoel, Sir Lanvai, Sir Lamorak, Sir Maleagant, Sir Pellinore, Sir Sagramore, Sir Urien."

He turned to Junipa.

"Now let me tell you the plan."

He quickly outlined what he intended they should do.

"Still doubtful?"

She still could think of nothing to say.

18

The Lord High Admiral of the Orsonian Battle Fleet felt a gnawing suspicion growing. Nullaborean secession was yet another problem to add to his list of worries, but there was something more. It wasn't anything he could put his finger on, but he felt as if the ground was shifting beneath his feet. He decided that he some needed advice. He could not call in a trusted adviser, because that was a certain precursor to assassination. So he decided to call in someone that he could not trust at all, his deputy, the Vice Admiral.

He struggled to suppress feelings of contempt and distaste as the Vice Admiral entered.

"Good to see you as always, Vice Admiral."

"Always at your service, Lord High Admiral," replied the Vice Admiral, likewise struggling to suppress feelings of contempt and distaste.

"I thought we might have a little chat about the state of … ," he hesitated, "things," said the Admiral.

"Things, Lord High Admiral?" replied the Vice Admiral.

"Yes, you know, things. For example, how is morale in the Fleet?"

"Absolutely splendid, Lord High Admiral. Couldn't be higher."

"And what about the populace? I know we have had a few minor difficulties of late, but are they still with me?"

"Absolutely loyal, every one of them, Lord High Admiral."

The Vice Admiral knew that the Lord High Admiral must think things were bad if he was asking those questions.

The Lord High Admiral knew that things were bad if the Vice Admiral was giving him those answers.

"So no problems?" said the Admiral.

"Nothing we can't handle. Just a minor outbreak of populism."

The Admiral frowned.

"Populism? What's that? Some sort of disease?"

"You might call it that, Lord High Admiral. It's a social disease. A few malcontents complaining about the rich and religion. As head of the Orsonian Secret Police, I can assure you that we have it well under control."

"I should hope so, Vice Admiral. Keep me informed."

"Of course, Lord High Admiral."

The Vice Admiral smiled inwardly. He would secretly encourage the populist tide to rise until it made the Admiral's position untenable and then, as head of the Secret Police, he would smash it and take over. The power he had always desired would be his. He eyed the pictures of the Admiral's many wives and mistresses, contemplating which he would take.

.

Commander Splenditheran felt another gnawing suspicion grow. Nullarborean secession was yet another to add to his list of worries, but still there was something more. It wasn't anything he could put his finger on, but he felt as if the ground was shifting beneath his feet. He decided that he needed some more advice. On all previous occasions when he had needed advice, he had called upon the finest minds in the Southern Cross Federation to pool their collective wisdom. The strategy had proved uniformly useless – and, on occasions, disastrous. Fine minds were the last things that should be involved when matters of real importance were to be decided. So he decided to call upon one whose mind was anything but fine: his Chief of Staff. His combination of stupidity, obduracy and bloody-mindedness might be exactly what was required to analyse a tricky situation.

"Chief of Staff, I have called you in because I would like some advice."

There he goes again, thought the Chief of Staff, full of shit as usual.

"How can I help, Commander?"

"Things have been a little tricky of late. There is the Nullarborean situation, of course, and now the Financial Secretary of the Federation is saying that revenues have been falling and we are spending too much, particularly on the military. He is threatening to bring the matter to the Federation Council and is demanding savage cuts to all budgets, particularly the military budget. I don't need to spell out to you the consequences, especially with the Nullarborean situation being what it is. The military situation of the Southern Cross Federation would be jeopardized. What do you think we should do about him?"

Most of the time the Chief of Staff cared nothing for budgetary matters, but a threat to military purse strings was different. In the Chief of Staff's opinion there were two things that could sort out any tricky situation – a good weapon or a good brothel. He briefly contemplated having the Financial Secretary dematerialized, but decided that was no good. Another bean-counter would just replace him. He needed to be brought to heel. The Financial Secretary was a thin, balding individual with a whining voice, who leered at every passing female. The brothel was the answer.

"You need to get him caught with his trousers down, Commander."

"Pardon?"

"You need him to be involved in what I believe is called a compromising situation."

"How would we do that?"

"You catch him in a cathouse."

"Pardon?"

"You find him in a house of ill repute."

Splenditheran thought the idea mildly amusing, if unlikely.

"I cannot see the Financial Secretary in a brothel. He's not that sort."

"You need to get him well oiled."

"Pardon?"

"It's what we do in the military. If a soldier gets uppity, we get him rat-arsed, chuck him in a cathouse, then tip off the MPs, who drag him out while he's on the job. He's up before the commanding officer, does his chokey, and he's as good as gold after that. Works every time."

"You think you could do that with the Financial Secretary?"

"No problem. I know his sort. Probably never been laid in his life. We get a few pretty females around him and we pour the drink down his throat. I know just the little place to take him. The girls will have him every which way. You won't believe the pictures. He won't be able to look you in the eye after that. He'll do anything you say."

Splenditheran considered the idea. It was a rather different proposal from the many he had heard from the finest minds, but he was beginning to think that there might be something to be said for stupidity, obduracy and bloody-mindedness.

"I shall look forward to conversing with the Financial Secretary after he has enjoyed such hospitality, Chief of Staff."

The Chief of Staff was more than ever convinced that Splenditheran was full of shit, but he saw the upside. More money for the military meant there was a real chance of a proper war. The Orsonians were in need of a good hiding. He could hardly wait.

Civil Servant 21346 felt a gnawing suspicion growing. It wasn't anything he could put his finger on, but he felt as if the ground was shifting beneath his feet. The authors of the Populist Manifesto had contacted him, or so he thought. He had set up what was supposed to be a secret channel and through it came tracts detailing all the iniquities of Orsonian society and heralding the inevitable triumph of the downtrodden. There were claims that the movement was growing rapidly, with opposition to the elites breaking out everywhere, but he could see no evidence for it.

He had tentatively tried to spread the word among his fellow civil servants, but had been met with either indifference or incomprehension. Downtrodden they might be, but he was beginning to think that they didn't deserve uplifting.

He began to wonder if the movement was all that it seemed. Was he being manipulated? Certainly, things were becoming more risky, so he tried to convince himself that the greater the risk, the greater the reward. If he succeeded, then four of the Admiral's mistresses were not a sufficient reward. Eight was the least he deserved.

19

"I trust you will forgive our little misunderstanding, Sir Sechaverell."

The Great Sandjanum was at what he considered his most expansive best as he ushered de la Beche, Jim, Doctor Culpepper and the Knights into the great basilica of the Grand Kalaba.

"I'm afraid that those conniving idolators, the Sempiternal Ecclesia, had tricked me into believing that you had committed some offence against their ungodly practices. In a spirit of cooperation I had agreed to hand you over to them. I had no idea that you were a Knight of the Sacred Circle and, once I was so informed, I recognized how profoundly I had been deceived."

"Think nothing of it, darling," said de la Beche. "Don't blame yourself for having a trusting nature."

The Great Sandjanum's inclination to take offence at being so addressed was only partly assuaged by the compliments to his nature, but he decided to let things go.

"Most gracious of you, Sir Sechaverell. Now, let us proceed to the courtyard, where we have arranged a little celebration in your honour and where, I understand, the Knights are waiting to greet you."

He clapped his hands and together with several turbans and two sentries, the party descended the grand staircase and went out through two wide doors to the courtyard. Junipa slipped away and made her way to the kitchens, where she sidled up to Nimbolt, who was washing some large pans, and whispered to him.

"Nimbolt, you need to come with me now!"

"Why?"

"I've no time to explain. Just come."

They left the kitchen as discreetly as they could and went out into the courtyard, where Nimbolt was astonished to see the Knights on their steeds, drawn up in a line. The Great Sandjanum was addressing them.

"Knights of the Sacred Circle, may I welcome you to the Grand Kalaba in the name of Qudai, all blessings to him. I have the joyful task of reuniting you with your esteemed fellow Knight, Sir Sechaverell de la Beche. May you live long and continue with your great deeds in the fight for all that is good and holy."

Squire Squire stepped forward and raised his hand.

"Gentil knights, the high and mighty Great Sandjanum has thee welcomed to the Grand Kalaba and restored to us our well-beloved companion, Sir Sechaverell de la Beche. Be ye of great cheer to him."

The Knights all waved their swords and gave loud cheers.

The Great Sandjanum clapped his hands.

"In honour of this occasion, I have called for a feast: there will be songs and dancing for you to enjoy."

Within a very short time, tables had been brought out and food and drink put on them. The Great Sandjanum enjoined them all to sit. The Knights remained on their steeds.

"Would they not like to join us at the tables?" asked the Great Sandjanum.

"They prefer to stay mounted," said Squire Squire. "It's a bit awkward, clanking around in armour."

The Great Sandjanum nodded.

"I quite see that. The food and drink will be taken to them."

Jim surveyed the scene, glad to be out of the confines of the room. He watched as the Knights sat on their steeds, only stirring to take occasional draughts of drink. Then, out of a door, musicians, carrying instruments, appeared and began playing. Shortly after, the veiled dancers emerged and began their gyrations. Jim glanced again at the Knights, but they appeared as impassive as ever. Squire Squire, however, was watching intently, clearly fascinated by the dancers.

Jim found himself, as before, entranced by the combination of drink, food, music and the patterns weaved by the dancers. He was drifting into a reverie when, out of the corner of his eye, he saw Squire Squire lift his bugle to his lips and heard the rapid notes of a tattoo. Suddenly, the Knights dashed forward, drawing their swords. For a moment, the Great Sandjanum stood transfixed, as if not quite believing what he was seeing. Then he realized what was happening and yelled for his guards, who came pouring into the courtyard, axes at the ready, attempting to intercept the Knights.

"*A dexter*, Sir Esclabor!" yelled Squire Squire as one of the guards raised his axe, but before he could strike, the Knight cut him down with his sword. "*A sinister*, Sir Dagonet!" he yelled again: Sir Dagonet deftly removed the axe and the arm that had threatened him. Jim could see in the melee that the guards were no match for the battle-hardened Knights. They were falling like ninepins.

"Bravo," said de la Beche as another guard was felled. "Such *elan*. I must say, Knights do add tone to what would otherwise be a vulgar brawl."

As the remaining guards retreated, Squire Squire gave another blast on his bugle. A dozen Knights turned and sped towards the dancers, each scooping up a dancer and lifting her onto his donkey. Squire Squire ran towards the gates and, pushing a bemused Jovana aside, pulled the levers to open them.

Junipa shouted to de la Beche, Culpepper, Jim and Nimbolt to follow. They started to run after the Knights, dodging their way through prostrate, bleeding bodies.

The Knights with their dancers swept out of the courtyard, closely followed by Junipa and the others. Two remaining Knights turned back towards the gates and cut down any Qwezellaran guard foolish enough to follow them.

Squire Squire pointed to a carriage waiting on the road and shouted, "Get in that cab." They all piled in. "Follow those knights," ordered Squire Squire. The cabbie nodded and urged his donkey on.

"This is exciting," said the cabbie. "I've always wanted someone to say to me 'Follow that', but it's never happened before. What's up?"

"It's too complicated to explain," said Squire Squire. "Just keep going."

"Is it far?" asked the cabbie.

"It should take a few hours."

The cabbie pursed his lips.

"That's out of my normal area. I might not be able to take you. Even if I did, I'd have to charge you extra."

Squire Squire fixed him with a stare.

"You'll take us, if you know what's good for you. Did you see what the Knights did back there?"

"No. What?"

Squire Squire shook his head.

"Never mind. Just keep going. You'll get your money."

20

As they crested a hill, the castle came into view.

"I think I could become quite fond of castles," said de la Beche. "So much roomier than spaceships, though so much draughtier, too. It would need a complete change of wardrobe to keep out the cold. Now, darling," he said, turning to Squire Squire, "you have all these females on your hands. What are you going to do with them?"

"We'll have a tournament. The Knights can be their champions and woo them."

Junipa had no time for tournaments and wooing.

"That's just fantasy. What makes you think they want to be 'wooed', as you put it? We will take them to Penthiliope, of course."

"Why would they want to go there?" asked Squire Squire.

"Why would they not? They would be free from slavery, out of the clutches of all predatory males."

Squire Squire was far from convinced.

"I've known plenty of females only too keen to get into male clutches."

De la Beche saw Junipa was beginning to fume.

"Well, darlings, these are delicate matters. I don't think you should make any hasty decisions. A tournament might be a nice diversion from all our recent tribulations and, after that, everyone can make up their minds about what they want to do."

Squire Squire shrugged while Junipa looked doubtful. Then Nimbolt spoke.

"What about me? What can I do?"

Everyone turned to him. Squire Squire spoke first.

"I've been looking for an assistant. Do you fancy it?"

"What would your assistant do?"

"Assist me, of course."

Nimbolt persisted.

"How, exactly?"

"Organizing things; helping with feasts; polishing armour; watering and feeding the donkeys and shovelling – plenty of that."

"Shovelling?"

"Yes, donkey droppings. They are house-trained, but you know donkeys – they don't hold back."

"It sounds an ideal opportunity for a likely young fellow," said de la Beche. "Are there possibilities for promotion?"

"Naturally," replied Squire Squire. "I'm thinking of moving on soon. There are big opportunities for me in insurance. So he could take over as Squire and then Utrophia's his oyster."

De la Beche beamed.

"There you are, Nimbolt darling. Chances like that don't come along too often. What do you say?"

Jim saw Nimbolt swallow, as his gaze turned from Squire Squire to de la Beche and then back.

"Thank you."

***

Jim felt the breeze on his face as he sat in the large, multi-coloured tent. Next to him were Junipa, de la Beche and Doctor Culpepper and on either side were the dancers, now in bright, flowing robes and headdresses. He looked over the tilt yard as the first two Knights drew up in the lists. Squire Squire stood at the midpoint holding up a flag.

"Pret, Sir Brunor."

Sir Brunor raised his lance.

"Pret, Sir Maleagant."

Sir Maleagant, too, raised his lance.

"Avaunt!" cried Squire Squire, bringing down the flag with a flourish, as the two galloped towards each other.

Jim felt himself flinching as the two came together, but instead of the expected loud crash there was only a slight crack. Sir Brunor's lance had just clipped his opponent's shield, while Sir Maleagant had missed altogether.

They galloped to the ends of the lists and turned. Squire Squire again called "Pret" and then "Avaunt" and they came together once more. This time there was a louder crack, as both lances glanced off shields. They turned again and, at the signal, charged. Jim flinched as a very loud crack sounded as Sir Brunor's lance hit the middle of Sir Maleagant's shield, sending him crashing to the ground. Sir Brunor turned round, raising his lance in triumph, while Nimbolt ran out to help the winded Sir Maleagant to his feet.

"Conquereur, Sir Brunor," announced Squire Squire.

Jim heard a series of high-pitched sighs and exclamations. He looked along the line of dancers to see several drop small squares of cloth on the ground of the field. Sir Brunor removed his helmet to expose his flowing locks and rode over to the tent, picking up each piece of cloth with his lance. He pressed each to his lips, before waving and bowing to the dancers, to the accompaniment of more sighs and exclamations. Jim looked round at Junipa and could not decide whether her expression was one of astonishment or disgust. Then he heard a loud, deep roar and saw Sir Agravain approaching, waving a mailed fist. Sir Brunor jerked upright in his saddle and trotted smartly off the field, to the evident disappointment of the dancers. There followed an animated discussion between Sir Agravain and Squire Squire, before Squire Squire held up a large standard and announced that the tournament was at an end, and that they should all repair to the castle for the feast.

***

Jim, Doctor Culpepper, Junipa and Nimbolt were seated at their own table. Jim thought the feast was even more lavish than the last. A special table had been set for the dancers, who chatted excitedly among themselves, while giving coy glances towards the Knights. At the Knights' table he could see de la Beche seated in the Siege Perilous, next to Sir Agravain. The other Knights conversed and joshed as before, but Jim could see them glance occasionally towards the dancers; he could see, too, that Sir Agravain clearly disapproved.

Squire Squire came over to join them.

"Does Sir Agravain have a problem with the dancers?" asked Jim.

"Sir Agravain has a problem with lots of things," said Squire Squire. "He has a particular problem with females. He doesn't think they're good for discipline."

"He was keen enough to rescue them," pointed out Doctor Culpepper.

"Rescuing damsels in distress is one thing. That's what a Knight is supposed to do. But keeping them is quite another. Sir Agravain is old school, very old school. He doesn't believe in holding on to damsels once he's rescued them."

Junipa found herself surprised at approving the attitude of any male.

"Quite right. They must come to Penthiliope. It is the only way that they will be safe."

"I'm not sure they want to be safe," said Squire Squire.

Junipa bristled at the idea.

"Of course they want to be safe! Do you imagine that they want to stay here and be used in the same way that those slave-owning fanatics used them?"

It was Squire Squire's turn to bristle.

"Knights aren't like that."

Junipa snorted.

"Don't give me any guff about chivalry and codes of honour. That's just a veneer. All males are the same beneath the surface. They just want one thing and are prepared to do anything to get it."

There was a long pause before Squire Squire spoke again.

"You're wrong, but it doesn't matter anyway. Females aren't allowed on Utrophia and the word will be out soon – if it isn't already. They will have to go."

"I'm glad we agree," responded Junipa. "I will arrange for them to be picked up."

"Talking about going," said de la Beche, "I do feel in need of a little recuperation. I suggest we go back to the *Bountiful* for a wash and brush up. Then we can come back to continue the quest. Now Squire Squire, you seem to have your finger in every pie, is there someone or something that we could approach?"

Squire Squire pondered the question.

"I suppose you could talk to the Pantagnosts."

"The Pantagnosts? Who might they be?"

"They're a funny lot – polytheists. They believe in lots of gods. I've no idea how many. They have one for everything that you can think of and plenty more besides. Not that you could really call them gods. Their so-called gods fight, scream and screw like a bucketful of monkeys. Some Pantagnosts are just as mad, but they are a gabby lot and, if they know something, they would probably tell you."

21

The Lord High Admiral of the Orsonian Battle Fleet had never had much time for matters intellectual. "I'm a doer, rather than a thinker," he would say to anyone who could be made to listen. Doing was what he did. Thinking could be left to others since, in his opinion, very little good ever came of it. So, when an idea did occur to him, it hit him with the force of a thunderbolt. He had to tell someone about it.

"I have had an idea, Vice Admiral."

The Vice Admiral was unable to hide his astonishment.

"Really, Lord High Admiral?"

"Yes, really," said the Admiral, rather testily. "I think we need to do something about this pustulism that you mentioned at our last meeting."

"Populism, Lord High Admiral."

"Yes, that's what I said. I understand from you that the populace is feeling restless."

"It's only a few malcontents stirring up trouble, Lord High Admiral. We can easily deal with them."

The Admiral was unconvinced.

"Perhaps, but these things can get out of hand. We need to do something to take the populace's minds off things."

"Such as, Lord High Admiral?"

"Games, Vice Admiral."

"Games, Lord High Admiral?"

The Lord High Admiral was beginning to think that his deputy was developing the irritating habit of Civil Servant 21346, repeating everything he said.

"Yes, games. In the days of the old empire, emperors would entertain the populace with games and feasting. I think we need to revive the idea. It should combine appeals to the martial spirit with magnificent spectacle."

"That is indeed an excellent idea, Lord High Admiral. What exactly did you have in mind?"

The Admiral found his imagination beginning to soar.

"We should have re-enactments of the great victories in Orsonian history, culminating, of course, in my glorious victory over the Mandrinians. Then, for more spectacle, I suggest we revive something that happened in the earliest days of the empire – a bestiast!"

The Vice Admiral found himself baffled.

"Another excellent idea, Lord High Admiral."

The Admiral was now in full flow.

"A bestiast, as you know, involves sacrificing prisoners to fierce wild animals, so we will need plenty of both, if we are to have a proper spectacle. Prisoners will be no problem. We still hold plenty of Mandrinians, but what about wild animals? Do we have them?"

The Vice Admiral's bafflement increased.

"I expect so, Lord High Admiral, but I am afraid that wild animals do not come under the control of the military, so I cannot be absolutely sure."

The Lord High Admiral saw his point.

"I see your point, Vice Admiral. The military has better things to concern itself with than wild animals. Let us find out where we can get them."

Civil Servant 21346 found himself in front of the Lord High Admiral and Vice Admiral.

"Civil Servant 21346, I have been discussing an idea I have had with the Vice Admiral."

Civil Servant 21346 was well practised in hiding his astonishment, but, even so, he had to struggle.

"How may I be of assistance, Lord High Admiral?"

"This idea needs lots of fierce, wild animals. Where can we get them?"

Civil Servant 21346 gave up the struggle to hide his astonishment.

"Wild animals, Lord High Admiral? May I ask what they are for?"

The Admiral found his enthusiasm for his idea mounting ever higher.

"I intend to revive the ancient Orsonian tradition of the games, to uplift the spirits of the populace and take their minds off some seditious ideas that I understand a few malcontents have been peddling. The games will be full of glorious spectacles, one of which will be a bestiast, where prisoners are sent in to the arena with wild animals. We will need a lot of them."

Now it was *his* imagination with which Civil Servant 21346 struggled. His mind went almost blank.

"I understand that the Imperial Zoo has the finest collection of animals in the empire, Lord High Admiral."

The Admiral had vague memories of being taken round the zoo as a very young child and seeing fat, lazy carnivores lolling in the sun. He had something fiercer in mind.

"I had something fiercer in mind, Civil Servant 21346. Is there nowhere that we might find them?"

"Most planets have killed off all their wild animals, Lord High Admiral. The only ones left are in captivity."

The Admiral sighed.

"Then they will have to do. We will need to starve them for a bit to make them hungry."

Civil Servant 21346's presence of mind was returning. He was becoming alarmed.

"Are you saying that you want the animals to attack the prisoners, Lord High Admiral?"

"Not just attack them – devour them. That's the whole point. It will be a magnificent spectacle – on every screen on Orson. The populace will go wild with excitement. They will recover their martial spirits and Orson will be as one – as in the ancient days."

The idea was so absurd that it was almost bound to succeed. Civil Servant 21346 desperately tried to think of ways to stop it.

"What about the Conventions, Lord High Admiral?"

"What conventions?"

"The Galactic Conventions on prisoners of war that state that they may not be mistreated."

The Admiral had no time for bureaucratic niceties.

"Do these Conventions mention being devoured by wild animals?"

Civil Servant 21346 inwardly cursed the lack of imagination of those who drew up the Conventions.

"Possibly not, Lord High Admiral."

The Admiral jeered triumphantly

"There you are, Civil Servant 21346. If it's not mentioned, then it's not forbidden. That's the way these things work. The games will go ahead. I will appoint you, Vice Admiral, as head of the Organizing Committee. Civil Servant 21346 and his colleagues will assist you with all the preparations. With your great energy and enthusiasm, I am confident it will be the greatest spectacle Orson has ever seen."

The Vice Admiral just managed to reply.

"I'm sure it will be magnificent, Lord High Admiral."

The Admiral was now in full flow.

"After that, we must prepare for war with the Southern Cross Federation. The populace will demand it. No more shilly-shallying. We will show those insolent braggarts what the Orsonian Empire is made of."

Civil Servant 21346 felt his heart sink. All hope of escaping his dreary, loveless situation was beginning to vanish. The populace, its blood lust roused by the bestiast and the prospect of cheap victories, would revert to imperial type. Nothing would change. The old order would go on as always. The Lord High Admiral would remain triumphant. He stared at the floor, not noticing the sickly rictus of a smile spreading across the face of the Vice Admiral.

22

Back once more on HMS *Bountiful*, Jim stared, almost dazzled, at the image of a Bonhume scroll that he had transferred to a large screen. Highly-coloured and with lavish use of gold foil, it was covered in minutely-detailed drawings of fantastic beasts and plants, together with grotesque figures, male, female and inde-terminate gender, that seemed as if they were about to leap out from the scroll and attack him. At its top was the picture of a bearded figure in blue and red robes reading from a scroll. The script was particularly intricate, full of curlicues and serifs that made it very difficult to read. Eventually, after much effort, he began to decipher it.

The Necessity for Conflict in the Ludic Era

The reformulation of the laws of space-time in terms of hypercomplex dimensions[1] led directly to the development of hyperspace travel. As a result, much of the Galaxy was explored and all those places in causal connection with each other through hyperspace operated as if mutually at rest, and thus could be considered connected temporally in a time zone delineated as Universal Galactic Time (UGT).[2] Although all records of that era were apparently destroyed,[3] it seems reasonable to infer the events took a course not dissimilar to the following:

- Exploration of the Galaxy took place in a relatively short period of time.

- It is clear from genetic analysis that a single sentient race is the ancestor of all Galactic populations, although it is not clear exactly where the original population evolved.[4] If there were other sentient races on some planets, they were rapidly displaced or eliminated.

- The transfer of all knowledge and the control of all essential infrastructure to Inference Engines necessitated the protection of that information from corruption or theft. Consequently, Inference Engines protected their autonomy by preventing access to all data, technical and historical, deemed necessary to protecting their hegemony, in effect destroying all historical records.

- Lack of historical continuity led to isolation, fragmentation and the development of differing social, cultural and religious practices among Galactic populations.

- Periods of isolation have meant that there are now distinct genetic differences between some populations.[5]

Jim found himself fascinated by a group of figures, strung out across the scroll, that appeared to be engaged in some sort of ecstatic dance. With an effort he forced himself to continue reading.

Following on from the work of De'neev, Strengupan and others, J. F. Destrukondron and his co-workers at the Denebian Institute of Sociodynamics constructed an extensive theoretical framework that modelled social developments in interacting sentient populations.[6]

Their model showed that, given any reasonable boundary conditions, developments would almost inevitably follow a particular path:

- Almost all exploration would occur at or near the De'neev maximum, the time of greatest technological and intellectual development.

- Exploration and colonization are evidence of a psychic drive in the founding population that would have necessitated the suppression of any competing races.[7]

- The retreat from the intellectual and social values of the De'neev maximum towards forms of social and religious orthodoxy would have occurred at different rates. That would lead to what Destrukondron dubs the 'era of warring empires'. A society would gain some advantage in organization and weaponry and conquer its immediate neighbours. This would bring it into conflict with other societies that had acted similarly. The result would be further conquest. Eventually, one organization would rule over much of the Galaxy.

Destrukondron showed in a lapidary paper, "Modular Hegemonies in an Infinite Dimensional Semi-Numinous Manifold,"[8] that a single Galactic empire was inherently unstable and would inevitably break up into a number of elements. The equations proved that religious determinism was a necessary *and sufficient* condition for the consolidation of power by a ruling class in those elements and that such religions would trend asymptotically to the dogmatic and hierarchical. They showed, too, that conflict was inevitable for societies with differing and incompatible religious beliefs. Such conflicts, if unconstrained, would be extremely destructive. For equilibrium it was therefore necessary for warfare to be ritualized, limited in its destruction and confined to peripheral areas. Rulers could use conflicts to enhance their prestige and rally their populations, but in reality any gains or losses would be small and inconsequential. In essence, warfare would become a continuous game in what Destrukondron called the *"Ludic Era"*.

References

1. Using hypercomplex dimensions, expressed in octonion form, means recasting the equations of space-time in complex sixteen-space instead of four-space.

2. For a definitive account of the efforts to establish an agreed UGT see *Out of Time, Out of Mind* by G. F. Scroptic, Orion Nebula Press.

3. The first editors of *Principia Ontologica* did collect a number of documents that were thought to originate from the early history of Galactic exploration, but are now believed to be forgeries.

4. A number of planets have claimed that they were the site of sentient evolution. None of these claims has been accepted.

5. Many, if not most, races are believed to be co-fertile, although religious taboos, ethics and matters of taste prevent this question from being assessed.

6. See J. F. Destrukondron *et al.*, *Elements of Sociodynamics*, DUP.

7. No trace of previous sentient populations has been found, although it is possible that such traces were destroyed.

8, *Proc Gal Sci Soc*, xiii, iv, pp 578-609.

Jim recalled that the *Princ Ont* had also mentioned the Ludic era. Was everything a game? If so, who was playing and was there a referee?

23

The grave countenance of Ecclesiarch Adeodatus looked down on them from his throne.

"Reverends Jonah, Maggie and Dick, I fear I have sad news for you. The heretic and blasphemer de la Beche has been allowed to escape by the infidel Qwezellarans. He is now believed to be in the clutches of the Knights of the Sacred Circle."

The three looked stunned.

"Knights of what?" said Maggie.

"Knights of the Sacred Circle. They are a pack of renegades, who claim holy purposes, but in reality are prepared to offer their services to anyone who cares to pay for them."

Maggie could feel that Sloakum was about to explode, muttering under his breath how he would blast every knight – whatever a knight might be – to sub-atomic mush, entirely forgetting that none of those weapons worked on Utrophia. She gave him a sly kick.

"That is bad news, Yer Worship. Could we not go and get him from those Knights?"

The Ecclesiarch shook his head.

"Unfortunately, they are skilled in armed combat, so it is unwise to oppose them directly."

"What about talking to them?" said Maggie. "You said they like a fee. Maybe we could buy him off them."

The Ecclesiarch shook his head again.

"I'm afraid that is not possible. Somehow, this de la Beche has been inducted into their Circle. He is now one of their Knights and so they could not give him up."

"Are ye saying that there's nothing to be done?"

"Unfortunately, I can see nothing at present. However, I do have some good news for you."

The three exchanged glances.

"Good news, Yer Worship?" said Sloakum.

"Yes. I have been in conclave with my Ordinals, and we have decided that the wandering ministry of the Alcocatamites should now come to an end. You have pursued your holy ministry magnificently, and your reward shall be a secure retreat, away from all the troubles and demands of this world, so that you can spend the rest of your days in prayer and contemplation."

The looked at each other, utterly bemused.

"Pardon, Yer Worship?" said Maggie.

Adeodatus gave them his most benevolent smile.

"A special priory has been reserved for you, with its own chaplains. You will be pleased to know that I have consulted our most eminent theologians and they believe that they have discovered the principles of mortification of the flesh by cat o' nine tails, by which you place such store. The chaplains will administer it to you daily, so that your place in Paradise is absolutely assured."

Maggie felt the beginnings of panic.

"Very kind of ye, I'm sure, Yer Worship, but I don't think we're ready for that yet."

Adeodatus continued to smile benevolently.

"As your religious superior, I am the judge of whether you are ready or not – and I judge that you are ready. As good and true Alcocatamites, you have no choice but to obey me. Not to obey would mean that you would be a heretic, with all that entails. You will go to your retreat. It is for the good of your souls."

24

Jim examined the last image he had taken of the Bonhume scrolls. It was covered with drawings of fantastical animals, flying, running, leaping, swimming and occasionally devouring each other. Reading the scrolls had become a little easier, but understanding them had most definitely become harder. This one seemed to him the most impenetrable of the lot. Who wrote them, why had they been written and what, if anything, did they mean?

The Concentration of Reason

Classically, information theories assumed that, under any likely conditions, singularities, where all information is held centrally by some entity, were either impossible or unstable. Information was inherently "leaky" and transmissibility would always exceed any constraining force. However Squawking and Codrose,[1] by treating information as connecting nodes in an infinite-dimension Riemannian manifold, showed that, under any reasonable energy conditions, geodesic incompleteness occurs when information is concentrated beyond a certain point and a singularity inevitably results.

References

1 S.F.Squawking and R.G. Codrose, *The Large Scale Structure of Information*, Proc Den Sci Soc, vii, pp 321-96.

The Quantification of Unreason

Ligutrobe and Herfactil[1] have proved that there is no exact
solution to the General Equation of Sociopolitical Systems that
relies on information-processing alone, when concentration of
information approaches the asymptotic limit of a singularity.[2]
Exact solutions are impossible, even in principle, since they
would require initial conditions to be specified to limits beyond
the Planck scale. Even for approximate solutions, standard
perturbation theory approaches lead to diverging outcomes, so
that information and energy requirements for surveillance and
control rapidly exceed any feasible limits when the number of
sociopolitical units is much less than the current number of
such units in the Galaxy.

Jim's eye was caught at the bottom of the scroll by the depic-
tion of a long, scaly creature, dragon-like, with two set of wings
and a dozen or more legs, busily devouring a figure whose head and
arms could be seen disappearing down its throat. What did any of it
mean? He no idea, so he decided to read on.

Consequently, the General Equation is non-linear and
chaotic at all dimensions and scales, but, in certain subsets
of phase space, the chaotic behaviour that takes place
exhibits strange attractors of sub-Lorentzian type. These
could be considered, in effect, islands of quasi-stability
within the phase space occupied by the attractor, but,
since solutions are very sensitive to initial conditions, there
is a large, possibly indeterminate, number of solutions to
the equation, each exhibiting its own attractor. Ligutrobe
and Herfactil[3] have further shown that the following are
necessary, *but not sufficient,* conditions for quasi-stable
solutions:

- The number of competing political units must be greater than $2\pi^2N$ where N is the number of causally connected polities.

- Each political unit must cultivate an indigenous and exclusive religion, having a faith to rationality ratio that exceeds 10.

- Each political unit must exhibit coefficients of inequality and stratification greater than 0.85, where 1 is the maximum.

- Each political unit requires a male-female dominance ratio greater than 9.5, to ensure strict separation of functions for each gender and the supremacy of males in all functions except the domestic.

Jim looked at the illustration to see if it could be any guide to the text. A group of giant fishes, dressed in multi-coloured robes, gazed upwards, as if looking for revelation, while a winged figure floated above them. It didn't help. He resumed reading.

Ligutrobe and Herfactil were able to show that under these conditions any quasi-stable solution would include:

- The emergence of hierarchical secular and religious ruling classes, largely immune from challenge.

- The close identification of a religious hierarchy with a secular ruling class and the close coordination of punishments for deviation from either religious or secular norms.

- The covert promotion of a small clerical elite that would challenge the existing moral and intellectual order. This allows the identification of dissenting elements that inevitably emerge in any social system.

They would be isolated in quasi-monastic institutions and subject to ridicule on occasions, when necessary to deflect the populace from questioning the ruling order.

- The covert promotion of an unruly, quasi-criminal underclass, both to discipline any deviants from orthodoxy and to act as a scapegoat in the case of errors by the ruling classes. It could be culled periodically to reinforce moral codes.

- The fetishization of female virtue, involving strict dress and behaviour codes and separation of the genders in all social roles.

Using topological methods, ig-Tefmon and Vergoblik have extended the results of Ligutrobe and Herfactil in more rigorous fashion. Among their results are the laws of the *Sociodynamics of Fully Enclosed Multitheistic Systems:*

First law: Deities can neither be created nor destroyed. They can only change form.

Second law: When deities change form, disorder (theoentropy) increases.

Third law: The theoentropy of the system approaches a constant (residual) value when all interaction between deities ceases.

From this they were able to show that:

- Warfare between societies of differing theistic systems was inevitable and desirable within certain limits.

- Information concentration at, or asymptotically close to, a singularity enabled limits to be set on levels of warfare, where the probability of limits being exceeded in any particular case was inversely proportional to the tightness of those limits.

References

1. H.D. Ligutrobe and L.V. Herfactil, *Principles of Mathematical Sociopolitics*, Denebian University Press, pp. 675-87.

2. A singularity is defined as a monopoly of information coupled with the minimum level of knowledge capable of exerting control over everything specified in the information. Descriptions in this instance such as "superintelligence" are meaningless, since no sentient entity is capable of devising tests which distinguish whether another entity is more intelligent or simply in possession of more knowledge.

3. H.D. Ligutrobe and L.V. Herfactil, *A Supersymmetric Theory of Stochastic Dynamics in Multi-variant non-Equilibrium Systems*, Proc Gal Sci Soc, vii, pp. 543-61.

4. G.H.K. ig-Tefmon and Z. Vergoblik, *A Topological Theory of Warfare and Civil Strife*. Proc Ald Phys Soc, xxvii, pp. 345-78.

Jim stared at the scroll, eyes wilting under the strain of reading the intricately curling script. Even rereading it twice, he had only a faint idea of what it meant. Where did the text come from? Was it part of *Galactopedia* that had been lost, maybe even suppressed? Was it from the *Principia Ontologica*? Did it argue that wars were inevitable? Hardly a revelation. Was it implying that religions had their differences? Even less of a revelation. Or were the words largely meaningless, only a set on which the Bonhumes displayed their artistic virtuosity? He turned to another scroll that appeared to be connected to it. Certainly, the same hand had illustrated both, with the same fantastic beasts and figures festooned over it.

The Validation of Unreason

Nigutod and Begraftol[1] have shown that a single law is an emergent property of all sociopolitical systems whose complexity exceeds the Rescresci minimum.[2].A subset of it was first enunciated as Gresham's Law, in the study of what was once called Economics. It stated that *bad money drives out good*. A number of variants and generalizations of Gresham's Law applying in other fields have been put forward and Nigutod and Begraftol have been able to subsume these into a rigorously derived *Law of Unverification*. This states that *unverification drives out verification*. The number of sociopolitical assertions that can be verified (N_v) will always be less than the number that assert its opposite (N_u), and that consequently those who believe the opposite of any verifiable assertion will always be more numerous than those who believe it. Nigutod and Begraftol further show that, for any verifiable assertion, if $N_u > \Omega N_v$ (where Ω is the Nigutod-Begraftol coefficient[3]), then it is not likely to receive acceptance in any given situation. Consequences of this law include:

- There can never be agreement on the factual basis of any dispute concerning politics, financial matters or the law. What is fact to one side will be fake or nonsense to the other. Consequently any resolution of such disputes can only be by the exercise of power.

- Beliefs based on revelation or instinct, often of a religious nature, always override those based on empirical enquiry.

- Since there can be no agreement on what has happened, the power of history is enormously increased and becomes myth, a tale shaped entirely by those who create it.

References

1. K.T. Nigutod and V.B.Q. Begraftol, *Non-Euclidean Vector Formalisms in Sociopolitical Phase Space*, Fornax Monographs, xxvi, pp. 34-209.

2. The Rescresci minimum normally implies a faith to rationality ratio > 10 and a stratification ratio > 0.9. For a more rigorous derivation see Z.X. Rescresci et al., *The Ergodic Principle in Statistical Sociopolitics*, Pluto Press, pp. 456-532.

3. Ω is case dependent and is normally in the range $2 < \Omega < 10$, although it can approach zero in certain instances, such as those asserting the existence or otherwise of a deity.

Again, Jim reread the scroll, and again found himself bemused. Was it suggesting that nothing was true or merely that nothing could be agreed to be true? Were things only true if he thought they were true? He thought not. But on the other hand he only *thought* not. Maybe thinking was the problem. He stopped thinking and turned his attention back to the scroll. In the margin a creature with the head of a dog and the body of a human was attempting to mount a nude female. Was her expression agony or ecstasy? He couldn't decide.

Jim turned from the scroll and looked at the big screen. It was showing land dotted with a number of buildings, some large, some small, some bedomed, others flanked by columns.

"Any idea what those buildings are, Mister Betelgeuse?" asked de la Beche.

"I believe they are temples, Captain."

De la Beche looked back at the screen.

"I must say their god does seem a little self-indulgent, needing all those temples."

"I think you mean gods, Captain," said Mister Betelgeuse. "I believe this is the region occupied by the Pantagnosts. They are polytheists. I suspect that each temple is devoted to a particular god."

De la Beche pondered for a few seconds.

"Pantagnosts? Jim, didn't Squire Squire say we should talk to them?"

Jim nodded.

"Yes, Captain, but he didn't think much of them. He seemed to think their gods weren't really gods, just spoiled brats."

De la Beche smiled.

"Well, that makes a change from all those other gods, who do tend to take themselves a tad too seriously. I think we might take up Squire Squire's suggestion. They may be as profligate with their information as they are with their deities."

He thought for a few seconds. "What does one wear when visiting polytheists?"

25

The cutter set them down a short distance from one of the smaller temples, which appeared to be on the outskirts of the collection. De la Beche strode towards it. He was wearing a jumpsuit with vertical stripes of every colour of the rainbow, a gold and silver embroidered cape and an indigo cocked hat, topped with plumes. "I believe gods all have their favourite colour, darling," he had said to Jim, who was gazing transfixed. "It would not do to disappoint any of them."

The temple portico had several white columns and a frieze above that appeared to show a number of figures engaged in some sort of combat. As they approached, they saw nobody except a bewhiskered old man, who was sweeping the steps of the temple with a large broom. As he saw them, he stood up and waved the broom.

"You can't come in. Nothing on today. The auguries won't have it."

"Pardon, darling," said de la Beche. "Not quite sure I got that."

"I said," said the old man, slowly and deliberately, "you can't come in. The auguries won't have it."

De la Beche gave him a smile.

"I'm not quite sure we did actually want to come in, but who are these auguries who seem to making life such a misery for you? Perhaps I could have a word with them?"

The old man looked at him in disbelief.

"The auguries aren't a who. They're up there," he said, pointing to the sky.

"Up there?"

"Yes. There was a flight of lesser-striped parakots flying north in an inverted vee formation this morning. Nothing good can come of that."

De la Beche gave him a quizzical look.

"I'm sorry to hear that. What can a few birds do to you?"

"It's not what they do. It's what they portend – doom."

"Doom?"

"Yes, doom. The High Augurist has locked himself in the Sacristorium. He won't come out until goobies are seen flying south in double crux formation."

De la Beche surveyed the sky.

"No sign of any birds, I'm afraid. Oh, wait. What's that?"

Jim caught a glimpse of a small brown bird disappearing into a nearby bush.

"That's just a common dripe," said the old man, a note of contempt in his voice. "Dripes are no good for auguries. It has to be dreagles or fultures or goobies or parakots. They're the ones for portents."

Doctor Culpepper found himself intrigued by the idea of avian soothsayers.

"You say that these birds can foretell the future. How exactly do they do it?"

The old man looked at him as if not quite believing what he was hearing.

"The gods send them, of course."

It was Culpepper's turn to express doubts.

"What gods?"

The old man looked at him in exasperation.

"All of them. This temple is devoted to the god Hyppoleon, who often sends parakots, especially when he's angry. Flying north in inverted vee formation means he's very angry. Bad things will happen until goobies are seen flying south."

De la Beche nodded sympathetically.

"That is unfortunate, darling. This Hyppoleon of yours seems a rather disagreeable sort. Couldn't you find one a bit more accommodating?"

The old man had a look of horror on his face.

"You can't talk about gods like that."

"No offence meant," said de la Beche apologetically. "Tell me about Hyppoleon. What does he do?"

The old man seemed to find his ignorance inexplicable.

"He is the god of the underworld, as everyone knows. If he is not well disposed to us, he wreaks his wrath upon us and sends earthquakes and volcanoes and plagues."

"And you think that this flight of parakots means that an earthquake might be coming?"

The old man nodded.

"Or a volcano or a plague."

De la Beche looked doubtful.

"We haven't noticed any volcanoes on this planet. How does he conjure them up?"

The old man looked at him again in disbelieving mode.

"Not here. This is Utrophia, the sacred planet. Hyppoleon would not create volcanoes here. I was talking about our planet, Laccadaemonia."

"My apologies. Nothing, of course, should be allowed to disturb the tranquillity of Utrophia. Is Laccadaemonia troubled by volcanoes?"

The old man nodded again.

"And by earthquakes and by plagues."

"That does seem rather tiresome. Is there nothing that can be done?"

The old man sighed.

"We can only hope. The High Augurist is at this very moment intoning the sacred orisons to Hyppoleon, begging his forgiveness for any offence that we might have caused him and asking him to stay his wrath. But, I fear," he said, his expression turning ever more doleful, "certain bodies have turned Hyppoleon against us, with their false entreaties and shameless lies."

"Really? Who would want to do such a thing?"

The old man pointed to a distant building.

"The Haruspiccers. In our mythology, Hyppoleon was in love with the beautiful goddess Frumosine, but she was seduced by the great god Jivanion, in the form of a hippogriph, and bore him a son, the demi-god Jormes. Now the Haruspiccers have concocted a false myth that Frumosine was cast off by Jivanion and wished to be reunited with Hyppoleon. They have erected a statue of Frumosine in their temple and, most sacrilegiously, have said they will place a statue of Hyppoleon beside her."

Doctor Culpepper didn't think he was quite following.

"Why should that make any difference to how Hyppoleon feels about you lot?"

Jim thought he saw the old man wince as Culpepper mentioned "you lot".

"Frumosine is very beautiful and gods do as they will, without reference to us. Hyppoleon may fall prey to the seductions of Frumosine and cease to offer his protection to us, as the Haruspiccers claim that the entrails portend."

Culpepper's puzzlement increased.

"Entrails?"

The old man shook his head, surprised by yet another show of ignorance.

"They sacrifice animals and examine the livers for signs of omens. Complete nonsense, of course. Who takes any notice of livers? Omens can only be read in the sky."

Doctor Culpepper raised his eyebrows and looked first at de la Beche and then at Jim. None of them said anything for a few seconds, then de la Beche spoke.

"I know what you mean about livers, darling. Personally, I've never been one for offal, although I do make an exception for *foie gras*."

The old man stared at him as if not quite understanding what he had said.

"They say that the livers can tell them the portents. I say it's nonsense, but you would be surprised how many are taken in by it. It gets those of us who can read the portents a bad name."

"I suppose it would," said de la Beche. "Is the practice of portent-reading common?"

The old man raised his hands.

"You would not credit how many there are in the portent business. Sometimes I think everyone is at it."

"Really?" said de la Beche. "How do they go about it."

"Where do I start?" replied the old man. "There are the oracles. The one at Mellonti, up there," he said, pointing to a distant mountain, "is dedicated to the god Nipolo. The other one, at Parelthi," he continued, pointing to a peak near to the first, "is dedicated to the god Androla. They despise each other, so, if you get bad news from one, you can go to the other and be sure of good news. Then there are the necromancers, the cleromancers, the hydromancers, the pyromancers and a good few others – charlatans, mainly. I'm afraid all too many are willing to believe rubbish if it's dressed up in fancy talk."

"That I can believe," said de la Beche. "You mentioned a number of gods. As a matter of interest, do you know how many there are?"

The old man shook his head.

"I have never bothered to count. It's not my business. I am devoted to Hyppoleon. If you want to know about all the other gods, you had better ask the Archpontifex."

"Perhaps we should," said de la Beche. "Who is the Archpontifex?"

"The Archpontifex," replied the old man, "is the Supreme Invigilator. He oversees all the temples and resolves all disputes between mortals and gods."

"Most interesting, darling," said de la Beche. "We are on a mission to find something that an associate of ours has lost. We think it may be on Utrophia. Is it possible that your Archpontifex might be able to help us?"

The old man looked doubtful.

"The Archpontifex is an invigilator, not a helper."

"We all have our little foibles, darling, but, from what you say, it does seem that he would know what is going on round here. How might we find him?"

The old man pointed towards a distant hill. Jim saw that a paved road ran in its direction.

"Two hours walk will take you there. He resides in the largest of all the temples."

As they departed, Jim turned to see the old man looking at them as if he thought they were mad.

***

The temple was huge. They approached along a wide avenue flanked by scores of statues. Jim presumed some were of gods, male and female, dressed and naked, some holding weapons. Others were of animals and creatures that he could not believe had ever existed. A few figures, that he assumed were devotees, could be seen, flitting to and fro, though none seemed to notice the trio. They mounted steps to find themselves in front of serried ranks of massive columns and a pair of equally massive open doors, through which Jim could see an interior with yet more columns and arches, all richly gilded.

At the entrance to the temple stood two sentries, bedecked in colourful uniforms and brass helmets. Each was holding a large axe. As they attempted to enter, the axes came down, barring their path.

"State your business," bellowed one of the sentries.

"No need to shout, darling," said de la Beche. "We thought we might take a look round your beautiful temple."

"Only those truly devoted to Jivanion are allowed to enter," bellowed the sentry, in a voice even louder than before.

De la Beche smiled.

"I quite understand. Please give my best wishes to Jivanion. I'm afraid that we have never been to this splendid place before, so we are not entirely familiar with all your ways. As a matter of fact I was hoping to have a chat with your Archpontifex, who I'm sure could enlighten us."

The sentries looked startled. One of them banged his axe against a large gong next to him. Jim felt the sound reverberate through him. Presently, two figures appeared, dressed in shirts that shimmered with orange and purple polka dot patterning.

"We are subpontifices of the Temple of Jivanion. What is your business?" said one of them sternly.

Jim saw de la Beche give his most ingratiating smile.

"As I was saying to your colleagues, we were hoping to have a chat with the Archpontifex."

The subpontifices looked at him sternly.

"You do not ask to see the Archpontifex," said one. "If His Utter Supremacy wishes to see you, he will send for you. Why should he do so?"

"Let me introduce myself," replied de la Beche, "I am Sir Sechaverall de la Beche, *bart*, Captain of HMS *Bountiful*, the renowned privateer. This is Doctor Culpepper, the renowned surgeon, and this is Jim, the cabin boy. We would like to talk to the Archpontifex on a matter that involves the most delicate of religious sensibilities."

"What are these matters?" said one of the subpontifices, his voice dripping with doubt.

"It concerns a missing object of great religious significance. I can say no more unless I can talk with the Archpontifex himself."

The subpontifices looked at each other. "Wait here," said one and went off, leaving the other to stand guard silently over them. In about ten minutes he returned. "Follow me."

Jim gazed in awe as they entered the temple. Marble columns rose high into the vaulted ceiling. Everywhere there were statues and bas reliefs, painted in dazzling colours and decorated with gold leaf. They were led through a side door into a high-ceilinged corridor and then into a large room. Around its walls were painted landscapes, in which figures in varying stages of undress cavorted. In the centre was a pool, with a fountain gushing water that sparkled in the light. Jim looked into the pool and saw silver and gold fishes swimming lazily, occasionally coming to the surface to gulp morsels that were being thrown to them by a figure reclining languidly on a long, low couch at the side of the pool. He assumed it must be the Archpontifex. He was dressed in a mauve, silken robe with a purple shawl draped around his shoulders and had what looked like a garland of leaves on his head. Around his neck was a gold chain and from it dangled a jewelled medallion. On each of his fingers were gold rings, encrusted with jewels that sparkled as he threw food. His eyes fixed on de la Beche, looking him up and down from head to toe several times, before he finally spoke.

"Love the outfit. You *must* give me the name of your tailor."

De la Beche smiled graciously at the compliment.

"Of course, Your Utter Supremacy. He's a little man called Sarton, who lives on a planet you will never have heard of. He has the most brilliant team of seamstresses working for him. You just give him your measurements and he comes up trumps every time. I'm never less than pleased to see what he sends me. He is always ready to serve those with taste and style, so I would be delighted to recommend you to him. And if I may essay a compliment of my own, your temple is simply magnificent. I've never seen anything more splendid."

It was the Archpontifex's turn to be gracious.

"Yes, we like to glorify our gods in style. They demand no less."

"One does get that impression," replied de la Beche. "You do seem to have plenty of gods to glorify. How many would there be?"

The Archpontifex seemed surprised, and perhaps a little affronted, at the question.

"I have no idea. We are polytheists. The whole point of polytheism is that we can have as many gods as we like. To count them would be in very poor taste."

He gestured to them to sit on the couches lining the pool. A robed attendant brought fruit and wine that he placed on an adjoining table.

"Gifts of the gods Matunda and Divai. Do partake."

Jim picked up a soft yellow fruit and bit into it. The sweet juice spurted out and ran down his chin, forcing him to wipe it with his sleeve.

"Now, what is it you wish to see me about?" asked the Archpontifex. "Be quick. I have to conduct a sacrifice to Jivanion later this evening. He becomes irritable if I am late."

"I would hate to keep Jivanion waiting, Your Utter Supremacy," replied de la Beche. "We thought you might be able to help us find a lost item sacred to some friends of ours. We believe it is somewhere on Utrophia."

The Archpontifex looked sceptical.

"What is this item?"

"It's called the Holy Kwokkah," replied de la Beche.

"The what?" said the Archpontifex in scornful tones. "Never heard of it. It doesn't sound very sacred to me. Who are these friends of yours?"

"They are called Nullarboreans."

"Never heard of them either," said the Archpontifex, scorn rising. "Are they monotheists?"

"I believe so," replied de la Beche.

The Archpontifex snorted.

"Thought so. That's monotheists for you. They only have one god, so, if they lose something of his, they think it's the end of the world. Woe and doom and more woe are all you ever get from monotheists. Their gods are either boring killjoys or murderous sadists. They are always looking to find ways of stopping anyone having a good time. Do you know what some of these monotheists claim? They say that their god can see into your mind and knows your innermost thoughts. What do you think of that, Captain?"

"It does sound a most unwarranted intrusion into one's personal privacy."

"Precisely. It's unforgivable in my opinion. Who wants a god that can do that? What's more, gods of the monotheists all desire to be *worshipped*. How selfish is that? Or maybe they're just insecure and want everyone to love them. That makes all monotheists sycophants and fawners. We would all prefer to be liked, but none of us demands to be actually worshipped, do we?"

"Certainly not, Your Utter Supremacy."

"Why anyone believes in them I have no idea. Polytheism is much more *fun*. We have lots of gods. If you don't like one there are plenty of others to choose from. Our gods don't demand to be worshipped. Most of them couldn't give a fig what mere mortals think of them. They betray each other, seduce each other and fight among themselves. I could tell you any number of tales of our gods that would make your hair stand on end. Take the great Jivanion himself, as an example. He once fell madly in love with a beautiful maiden, Dio, and swept her up into the clouds, where he ravished her. His wife, the goddess Lycthera, discovered the tryst and, in anger, turned Dio into a white gerwynd and appointed the many-eyed canid, Archon, to guard her. Jivanion in turn sent Metacles, his son by the nymph Perdomene, to rescue Dio. He tricked Archon into drinking a potion of the herb, torax, that sent him into a deep sleep, and beheaded him. Jivanion gave

Dio back her female form and she bore him a son and a daughter before he tired of her and married her off to Thybagoras, king of the ancient realm of Phelebes. I think you will agree, Captain, that is very different from all those monotheistic gods, who just sit there and gripe about everything."

De la Beche nodded.

"I do so agree. Contemplating the meaning of existence would put anyone in a bad mood."

The Archpontifex eyed him suspiciously.

"I do hope you are not trying to be profound, Captain. I abhor profundity."

"Perish the thought, Your Utter Supremacy. I always say that affecting profundity is the mark of a shallow mind. Superficiality is all, as far as I am concerned."

The Archpontifex looked stern.

"I'm very glad to hear it, Captain. Monotheists are always going on about how profound their understanding is of whatever it is they understand – as if that makes up for all their other deficiencies. They even have a name for it – theology."

"Is that so, Your Utter Supremacy? I take it you polytheists don't indulge in such practices?"

"Absolutely not, Captain. We have philosophers instead."

"Really? What do your philosophers do?"

Why they philosophize, of course," replied the Archpontifex, a little scornfully.

"About what?"

"They philosophize about anything they care to philosophize about. Our philosophers are renowned."

"Most interesting, Your Utter Supremacy. I take it you read a great deal of philosophy?"

The Archpontifex looked astonished.

"Certainly not. Nobody reads philosophy. Philosophers don't want anyone to read philosophy. They might be much less re-nowned if everybody knew what they philosophized."

De la Beche nodded.

"I do see that, but forgive me for asking, what use, then, is philosophy?"

The Archpontifex gave a knowing smile.

"It keeps the over-opinionated out of mischief, Captain. What could be more useful than that?"

De la Beche could only agree.

"I can only agree, Your Utter Supremacy. I do take your points about monotheists. I don't think anyone would describe the Nullarboreans as party people. However, the political situation in their neighbourhood is very delicate and finding the Kwokkah might help smooth things over."

The Archpontifex shrugged.

"I don't think I can help."

De la Beche turned to Culpepper and Jim, wondering if they had any suggestions. Just then he heard a sound that he thought was familiar. Jim, too, heard what sounded like music in the background.

"Excuse me, Your Utter Supremacy," said de la Beche, "but is that *Da tempeste il legno infranto* from Handel's *Giulio Cesare?*"

The Archpontifex looked astounded.

"I'm now convinced that you are no monotheist, Captain. How did you know that?"

De la Beche beamed.

"Handel is a particular favourite of mine. I have seen all his operas."

Jim saw astonishment, tinged with a little jealousy, on the face of the Archpontifex.

"All of them? Even *Floridante?*"

"Of course. I believe it was the only performance in the Galaxy for over a century. Rossane sang flat the whole time. Such a shame."

The Archpontifex rose to a sitting position and opened his arms.

"Well Captain, I'm sure that, as a fellow devotee of George Frideric Handel, you will be pleased to know that I have created him a god."

It was de la Beche's turn to be astonished.

"A god? You can do that?"

"Of course. As Archpontifex, I can make anyone a god. Few deserve the honour more than the divine George Frideric."

De la Beche clapped his hands together in delight.

"Such a divine idea, too. Count me as one of his greatest adherents."

The Archpontifex nodded in acknowledgement.

"I expect you would like to see his temple."

"Absolutely, Your Utter Supremacy. Nothing would give me greater pleasure."

The Archpontifex clapped his hands. Jim saw several of the sentries who had stopped them at the Temple appear. They formed a phalanx round the Archpontifex, who gestured to the party to follow. They went out through a side door and found themselves in a wide square flanked by several temples. They marched towards one whose exterior, Jim saw, was particularly richly adorned with cherubim and seraphim, playing harps, horns and other musical instruments. As they entered, Jim found himself looking up at a large, gilded statue of a bewigged figure, dressed in jacket and britches, seated at a desk and holding in one hand what looked like a feather. At the foot of the plinth were two lightly-clad figures, one male, the other female, entwined in each other's arms.

"A fitting monument to the god, don't you think Captain?" said the Archpontifex.

"Absolutely. I can think of no better," replied de la Beche.

The Archpontifex saw de la Beche's eyes turning to the two figures.

"I'm sure you recognize them, Captain. Cesare and Cleopatra, forever in love. Sets things off beautifully, don't you think?"

De la Beche beamed again.

"*Caro! Bella! Più amabile beltà*. The perfect touch."

"So glad you think so, Captain. We perform his works here regularly, with a special performance on the winter solstice."

"*The Messiah*?"

The Archpontifex looked surprised.

"Hardly, Captain. *The Messiah* reeks of monotheism. A lapse of taste by the divine Handel, I think you will agree."

"Of course, now you mention it."

"I suppose even a god has to run with the popular prejudice sometimes. No, it would be either *Orlando*, *Alessandro* or, of course, *Giulio Cesare*. And as a mark of our particular devotion to the god Handel," continued the Archpontifex, "we have built his temple next to that of the Virtual Virgins."

"Ah yes, the Virtuous Virgins," said de la Beche. "I'm sure George Frideric would feel honoured."

"Virtual Virgins, Captain, not Virtuous," said the Archpontifex, a slight note of reproof creeping into his voice, "though I am sure they are virtuous as well. As you know, females are not allowed on Utrophia, so the custodians of our sacred fire must be virtual – as is the fire."

"Of course, Your Utter Supremacy," said de la Beche. "Silly of me to have forgotten. Something else that might interest you is that I am hoping to finish Handel's lost opera, *Oedipus Rex*. I already have some sketches for the first two acts."

The Archpontifex's eyes lit up.

"How marvellous. Do remind me. What is the plot?"

"In a nutshell, Oedipus is born the son of a king but is left out to die on a mountain as a baby because of a prophecy that he will kill his father. He is rescued by a kindly shepherd and grows up far away, not knowing who he is. He comes back to the land of his birth, kills the king, his father, and marries the queen, his mother. When all is finally revealed, she kills herself and he puts his own eyes out."

The Archpontifex shook his head in wonder.

"How romantic. Simply perfect for an opera. When you have finished, you must send me the score. I shall have it put on here." He hesitated for a few seconds. "Are there any sopranos in it?"

De la Beche looked surprised.

"Yes, Jocasta, the queen. Keening does require high notes."

The Archpontifex nodded.

"I do see that, Captain. Might a counter-tenor do?"

"Possibly, but he would have to be exceptionally counter, if you see what I mean. I have some marvellous ideas for the death scene. They expire in each other's arms, as she kills herself and Oedipus puts out his eyes. The house will be in floods of tears."

"I'm sure it will," said the Archpontifex. "I think we should be able to manage one 'soprano'. There are some on this planet who have made, let us say, certain adjustments, to make sure that their voice stays high and pure. One of those could take the role. You must come to see it."

Jim saw de la Beche hesitate for a second.

"I would be delighted, Your Utter Supremacy. I shall look forward to it.   Meanwhile, there is our other business. As I mentioned, we are hoping to find the Kwokkah. Are you sure you can't help us?"

The Archpontifex looked doubtful.

"I would like to help you, Captain, but I'm not sure I can. I am the Archpontifex, not a finder of trifles."

De la Beche tried another tack.

"Have you ever heard of Roy Pesshe?"

Jim saw a look of surprise on the Archpontifex's face.

"Why do you ask?"

"We had heard that he might be able to help."

The Archpontifex pursed his lips and adopted a solemn expression.

"Ah yes, Roy Pesshe. I have heard the rumours."

"What rumours?"

"That there is someone called Roy Pesshe, who lives in a temple like no other on Utrophia."

"A temple like no other?"

"Yes. Those who claim to have seen it say that it has no columns or porticoes, but it has many sides that appear to change as you look at them. All nonsense in my opinion. They were probably suffering delusions as a result of imbibing intoxicating liquors."

"Almost certainly, Your Utter Supremacy. I've known plenty in a similar condition claiming to have seen the most fantastical things. However, it does sound curious. Do you have any idea where this temple can be found?"

The Archpontifex looked very doubtful.

"I am only going by rumours that, I repeat, Captain, are most unreliable. There is a road from here leaving to the north-west. Where it goes I do not know and have no wish to know. I am told it goes through lawless land, but those who claim to have seen this temple say it lies several leagues from here on that road."

26

Squire Squire could hardly believe what he was hearing.

"I can hardly believe what I'm hearing. The Madlands? Why do you want to go there?"

De la Beche smiled, a little condescendingly, Jim thought.

"Because we have been told that we may find Roy Pesshe there."

"Who told you that?"

"The Archpontifex."

Squire Squire snorted dismissively.

"What does he know?"

De la Beche smiled again, even more condescendingly.

"He knows enough to make George Frideric Handel a god, which puts him rather high in my personal pantheon. Besides, it's the only interesting lead we have at present."

Squire Squire remained dismissive.

"There's nothing there except a load of madmen."

"What do you mean, madmen?"

"Religious nutters. They've been chucked out by all their sects and now they just roam the country, causing trouble. You don't want to go there unarmed."

De la Beche was unmoved.

"Thank you for the warning, darling. I think we can manage to fend off the odd madman."

Squire Squire shook his head.

"You don't get it. Some of them hunt in packs. If you are definitely going, I think I had better come along too - and I'll bring a couple of the Knights with me."

***

They passed the temple of the Pantagnosts and took the road to the north-west. De la Beche, Doctor Culpepper, Jim and Squire Squire trudged ahead on foot. Sir Brunor and Sir Galeschin brought up the rear on their steeds. De la Beche was dressed in what he termed his "Morning Glory" – a gold lamé cape over an emerald-coloured jacket, mauve blouse and lapis-lazuli pantaloons.

The road was clearly very old. It was pitted with potholes and the edges were crumbling. The terrain became more desolate, mostly low scrub and grey-green grass. The few buildings were low, ramshackle huts; most seemed to be abandoned. As they passed through one collection of huts, Jim saw a wild-haired, almost naked figure run out clutching something that he realized with horror was a skeleton. The figure ran alongside jabbering and shaking the skeleton, which gyrated, as if animated, in a macabre dance. Squire Squire shouted something that Jim could not catch and the figure ran off, disappearing back into one of the huts.

"That's Mikkyu," said Squire Squire. "He's a cheerful sort really, but he does like to remind everyone about death and the impermanence of life. He's got a bit of a thing about it."

"Good for him, but I have to say I've seen better song and dance acts," said de la Beche.

Squire Squire grinned.

"They don't just make a song and dance out of death. Look over there."

Jim tuned his gaze to the side of the road and saw a robed figure sitting on its haunches, eating from a bowl. At first he thought there was nothing unusual and then suddenly recognized that the bowl was a skull.

"Food for thought," said Jim and burst out laughing. Doctor Culpepper guffawed too.

"Very droll, Jim," said de la Beche, but he remained straight-faced.

"There's plenty more where he comes from," said Squire Squire. "Let's hope we don't meet Stigmot. He goes around with a dead dog tied to his leg. Says it reminds everyone of the spiritual baggage that they carry though life. That's as maybe, but he stinks to high heaven. You can smell him coming a mile off."

Jim saw de la Beche's nose wrinkle in disgust. They rode on; the scrub became taller and thinker. Suddenly, out of the woods, a number of hooded figures appeared. Squire Squire yelled out.

"Avaunt Sir Brunor and Sir Galeschin."

The Knights galloped forward, lances raised. As they saw them coming, the figures turned to run. Most disappeared back into the woods, but one slipped and fell. Spotting him, Sir Brunor thrust his lance into his rump, pinning him to the ground. He lay there, screaming in pain and fury.

Squire Squire watched him wriggle for a while before finally saying "Mercei, Sir Brunor."

The Knight withdrew his lance and the screaming stopped, as the figure struggled to his feet and limped off, clutching his bleeding buttocks.

"Who were they?" asked de la Beche, as he watched the bleeding rear disappear.

"No idea," said Squire Squire. "There's lots of their sort out here – religious cast-offs. They call themselves names like 'Divine Warriors' and 'Wrath of God' and go about slitting throats in the name of whatever god they worship."

"Most interesting," said de la Beche. "Do you have any more such delights in store for us?"

Squire Squire grinned again.

"Lots. I'm surprised we haven't seen any of the possessed yet."

"Possessed?"

"Yes. They're supposed to be possessed by devils. It makes them do all sorts of things like speak in funny languages and curse and blaspheme. I think they're a bit of a hoot."

The road passed through a small ravine. Jim saw the Knights look up warily, but all seemed peaceful. They rode through and, as they came out, Jim saw at the side of the road a tall pillar, several metres high, with what seemed to be a platform on top.

"That's Simple Simon," said Squire Squire. "He lives up there."

This time it was Doctor Culpepper who asked the question that had occurred to them all.

"Why would he want to do that?"

"Well, a lot of people seem to think he's some sort of holy man. He was always being asked for his advice on the right prayer to do this or the right offering to get that done, so he got fed up and took himself up to the top of that pole and said he wasn't coming down again."

"What does he do up there and how does he live?" asked Jim.

Squire Squire shrugged.

"Well, he does holy things and people give him food and stuff. From what I hear, he doesn't go short."

Jim gazed up at the platform, but could see no sign of its inhabitant.

"Let's see if he'll talk to us," said Squire Squire. "Ahoy, Simon," he yelled. There was no answer, so Squire Squire yelled again. "Ahoy Simon. Are you there?"

This time there was a reply.

"Go away."

Jim watched as Squire Squire rummaged in his pack and pulled out a brown lump of something.

"I've got something for you, Simon," he yelled. "It's your favourite."

Jim saw a face, mostly obscured by long, straggly hair and an equally long, straggly beard, peer over the edge of the platform.

"What is it?"

"Cured ham, from the Knights' farm. You know you love it."

Simon disappeared then reappeared, dangling a bucket on a rope that he lowered to the ground.

"Put it in."

Squire Squire put the ham in the bucket and Simon began rapidly hauling it up again.

"How are you doing, Simon?"

"Mustn't grumble."

"Keeping well?"

"Funny you should ask. A couple of those do-gooders from the Holy Rollers gave me a dodgy meat pie the other day. Gave me the squits. I gave them a dose of their own medicine when they came back."

Squire Squire laughed.

"That's what I call Divine Retribution, Simon. Keep up the good work."

There was a muffled reply from Simon, who had evidently begun to enjoy the ham.

The party moved on. The road now wound through low, rounded hills. After an hour or so, Jim thought he heard an odd sound and saw something in the far distance moving towards them. "What's that?" he asked.

Squire Squire squinted and waited several seconds before replying.

"Looks like flagellants."

"Whatever are flagellants, darling?" said de la Beche.

Squire Squire shook his head.

"You'll see."

Jim watched as a procession of several dozen figures came towards them. He and the others moved off the road as the procession went past, seeming not to notice them. The noise was almost deafening, as well as utterly discordant. Some banged large drums, others blew long horns, while most chanted a dirgelike litany and continually scourged themselves across their backs with long chain flails.

They watched in silence as the procession disappeared along the road.

"Now I've seen them," said de la Beche, "I'm afraid I'm none the wiser. Do enlighten us. What do these flagellants think they are doing?"

"They're trying to stop the plague."

"What sort of plague?" said Doctor Culpepper. "I haven't seen any signs."

"How would I know? All sorts, I suppose," replied Squire Squire.

"Well, is there any sort of plague here?" said the Doctor.

"Not as far as I know."

"Has there ever been any plague on Utrophia?"

"Don't think so."

"So why do they do it?"

Squire Squire shrugged.

"They think it's working. If they stopped, the plague would come."

There was a momentary silence while they considered this.

"Exemplary logic, darling," said de la Beche. "Who could possibly disagree?"

They went on. Several hours later, they came to the crest of a hill. On the crest of the next hill, Jim saw something that looked like a large building. The more he stared at it, the more it seemed oddly familiar.

"I think we may have seen one of those before," said de la Beche.

It was a Tesseract.

The road seemed to lead directly to it. At one side of the road, just before the Tesseract, there was a large stone obelisk. As they came near, Jim saw that letters had been carved on its surface.

"Do your stuff, Jim, and read it for us," said de la Beche.

For a few seconds, Jim stared at the words, trying to gauge their meaning. Then he began to read.

God is all knowing

All knowledge is power

All power corrupts

Absolute power corrupts absolutely

Welcome to the house of God

27

Squire Squire eyed the building warily. The harder he stared, the more it seemed subtly to change its shape, although he could never quite work out what exactly had changed.

"Never seen anything like it."

De la Beche, too, was scrutinizing it.

"No sign of an entrance."

Squire Squire shook his head.

"We wouldn't go in there, even if there was."

De la Beche seemed surprised.

"Why not? What do you imagine is there?"

"Who knows? One rule of the Knights is never go into strange castles."

"Very wise, darling, I'm sure," said de la Beche, "but I'm afraid that we must try to find a way in. Let's take a look."

De la Beche, Doctor Culpepper and Jim walked forward until they were in touching distance. Jim put his hand on the wall. He could not decide what it was. Its matte surface was slightly warm to the touch. It was definitely not metal, but nor did it feel quite like stone. Just as he was about to take his hand away, there was a flash. For several seconds he was dazed, not quite understanding what had happened. Then he realized that he, de la Beche and Doctor Culpepper were standing inside a large grey-walled room. It was illuminated by a low, diffuse light, though he couldn't see the source. He turned to de la Beche, whose expression registered only the slightest sign of surprise.

"It seems we are in, darlings, whether we like it or not. What next?"

"We may be in, Sechy," said Doctor Culpepper, "but is there any way out?"

As Jim's eyes became accustomed to the gloom he saw writing illuminated on the opposite wall.

What is the past?
The past is unknowable.

What is the future?
The future is unalterable.

What is the present?
Between the past and the future
there is no present.

De la Beche saw it, too.

"Very gnomic. Perhaps it's one of those profundities that the Archpontifex so abhorred. If so, I'm with him."

Then, in the corner, Jim saw something else. He stared hard to make sure he was not mistaken, but there was no mistaking the flat features of Grosse Calabi-Yau. As the gloom began to lift, Jim could see he was lying on a richly carved divan. He slowly took a hookah from his lips and looked back at them with something like a sneer.

"Is there no escaping you?"

There was silence for a few seconds, before de la Beche replied.

"I could say much the same to you, darling. How do you come to be here? The last we saw of you was on Libertania."

Grosse waved the hookah hose dismissively.

"We are not constrained by mere spatial considerations, unlike those of you so dimensionally impoverished. We are anywhere and everywhere."

De la Beche smiled benignly.

"Aren't you the lucky one, darling?" He looked around the bare room. "And I suppose the Tesseract is anywhere and everywhere as well?"

Again, Grosse waved the hookah dismissively.

"'Where' is not a word we use when discussing the Tesseract. It is far beyond 'where'."

Jim decided to intervene.

"When I last saw you, you told me to seek Roy Pesshe. We have been told that he might be here. Is that true?"

Grosse took several puffs on the hookah. Jim stared at him, but still could not work out what happened to the smoke. Eventually, he spoke.

"To find the answer to that question you must pass the tests."

The three looked at each other.

"What tests?" asked the Doctor.

Grosse waved the mouthpiece of the hookah in the direction of the far wall. "Start with that little riddle," and then he slowly faded away. They looked towards the wall and saw that what was written on it had changed.

Which of these are equivalent?
1. *The incompleteness theorem*
2. *The uncertainty principle*
3. *The second law of Thermodynamics*

Beside each was a small green button that flashed. De la Beche gave a snort.

"Someone is having a joke at our expense. This goes beyond profundity to fatuity."

Jim stared at the writing. He had no idea what it meant.

"Maybe if we choose the right answer we might get out of here."

De la Beche snorted again, but the Doctor thought Jim might have a point.

"It's worth a try, Sechy. What's to lose?"

De la Beche waved his hand dismissively.

"Answer what, exactly? What incompleteness theorem? I'm completely in the dark. Uncertainty as a principle? That sounds like a contradiction in terms. As for the laws of Thermodynamics or anything else, you know my opinion of laws – for the obedience of fools and the avoidance of anyone with an ounce of sense."

The Doctor nodded.

"I take your point, Sechy. I know you're not a big fan of laws, but I'm not sure you can avoid the second law of Thermodynamics. It's a bit like gravity. You're stuck with it."

Jim wasn't sure about the second law of Thermodynamics either. Maybe it was incomplete, or perhaps uncertain.

"Maybe they're all the same and that's what we should choose."

De la Beche shrugged.

"Go ahead."

Jim pressed each of the buttons. In an instant, walls, room and everything disappeared. Instead, they found themselves looking from a distance at what seemed to be a turreted stone castle, rather like that of the Knights of the Sacred Circle. In front of the castle was a lake, on which a figure in a small boat rowed slowly towards the shore. Jim felt a flash of recognition as he watched the balding, bearded figure step out of the boat, carrying a long stick, and walking with a distinct limp towards the castle.

"It's the Coder, the one I saw on Libertania."

The other two looked at him in surprise.

"Are you sure Jim?" asked the Doctor.

"It's either him or someone who looks exactly like him."

De la Beche remained sceptical.

"I'm sure you have convinced yourself, Jim, but what would he be doing here? From what you told us, these Coders are not in the religious business."

Jim had to confess he had no idea.

"That's true, but Grosse seemed to say that the Tesseract on Libertania and here are the same. Maybe they have the same sort of person inside."

De la Beche's scepticism had not diminished.

"Maybe, Jim, but then again, maybe not. Besides, where is the Tesseract now? It seems to come and go as it pleases."

The Doctor nodded.

"So it does, Sechy, but we are where we are – wherever that may be. Why don't we try to get into that castle and see if Jim is right?"

De la Beche assented grudgingly. They walked towards the castle and approached a large wooden door. On one side was a brass handle. Jim pushed down on it. It gave and the door swung open, creaking loudly. They peered inside, but could see little in the gloom. Then they heard a loud voice.

"Who dares enter Castle Qarbonik?"

As his eyes became more accustomed to the light, Jim became aware of something in the corner of the room. At first he could not make out what it was, but, as he stared harder, he saw to his astonishment that it was a creature that had the head and neck of a snake, a hairy, spotted body like that of a large carnivore and cloven hooves like those he had once seen on farm animals.

For several seconds they gazed at it, almost disbelieving. The light was now brightening; Jim found himself staring at the iridescent yellow and green scaly skin of the creature's head, its wide, gaping mouth, with its rows of pointed teeth, its flickering, forked tongue and its huge eyes, with eyelids that opened and closed sideways. De la Beche broke the silence.

"Apologies for the intrusion, darling. Allow me to introduce ourselves. I am Sir Sechaverell de la Beche, *bart*, Captain of the privateer, HMS *Bountiful*, this is our physician, Doctor Cuthbert Culpepper, and this is Jim, the cabin boy."

"Well," said the creature, "what do you want? Be quick about it. Can't you see I'm busy?"

Jim looked around, but could see no obvious sign of busyness.

"With whom do I have the pleasure of speaking?" said de la Beche.

The creature gave a derisive snort.

"I am the Questing Beast, the Guardian of Castle Qarbonik. I thought everyone knew that."

"Most remiss of us, I'm sure," said de la Beche apologetically. "I'm afraid we have led rather sheltered lives."

The creature looked at them sternly.

"I'm not sure I believe that those are your names. Are any of you called George?"

"George?"

"Yes, George, and have you brought swords and lances?"

De la Beche shook his head, puzzled.

"I can assure you, darling, no Georges, no lances and no swords. Why do you ask?"

The Beast snorted again.

"I've had a number of Georges turning up here, with their swords and lances, wanting to slay me. I sent them all packing, I don't mind telling you."

De la Beche smiled sympathetically.

"Enough to put you off Georges for life, I'm sure, but we are entirely peaceful. Now, did I catch your name correctly – the Questing Beast?"

"Yes," replied the creature. "As I said, I am the Questing Beast."

May I ask," said de la Beche, "what it is you quest?"

The Beast made a noise that sounded to Jim like a cross between a snort and a cough.

"I cannot say. They are things that are unknown and unknowable to you, but they are such things that are the terrors of the Galaxy." He gave them another unblinking stare. "I see that you are not terrors of the Galaxy, merely a bunch of ne'er do wells, so you had best be gone, lest I send you packing, like all the Georges."

"No need for insults, darling," said de la Beche. "I do think you are being a little hasty. Appearances can be deceptive. After all, you're hardly a picture yourself."

It was the Beast's turn to be affronted.

"What do you mean?"

"Take a look at yourself – all bits and pieces. Who or what could possibly have been your parents? And what *were* they thinking when they had you?"

The Beast, clearly annoyed, drew its head up and back, its tongue flicking in and out.

"I have no need of parents! I am a mythological beast."

There was a pause, as the three digested this.

"What exactly do you mean by mythological?" said Doctor Culpepper.

"I mean," said the Beast, in what Jim thought was a surprised tone, "that I am mythical. I do not exist."

"But I can see you and hear you," Jim blurted out, before the others could reply. "How can you say you don't exist?"

The Beast gave another snort-cough.

"You can see me and hear me because you believe in things that don't exist, of course."

Jim was taken aback – and not a little insulted.

"That's silly. Of course I don't believe in things that don't exist."

"What makes you so different?" said the Beast in condescending tones. "Everyone else does. Belief in things that don't exist is absolutely rampant on Utrophia. You can hardly move for things that don't exist here."

Jim had to admit that there was something in what the Beast had said. He thought back to the Paradox Cafe when Ad had, rather unfairly he thought, cast doubt on whether Jim existed.

"I was once told that I didn't exist. What do you make of that?"

The Beast's eyes seemed to narrow and his tongue darted out several times before he answered.

"You were misinformed," said the Beast. "You are doomed to exist."

"Why doomed?" said Jim, puzzled.

"Everything that exists must come to an end," replied the Beast. "We who do not exist are immortal."

Jim recalled the sayings of Red, Ad and Abs in the Paradox Cafe and how he knew that they must be nonsense, but couldn't quite see why. He was beginning to suspect that this was another of that sort. Then, an idea occurred to him.

"I think I know how to make you exist."

"Hah!" said the Beast, flicking its tongue contemptuously. "What do you know?"

"Well," replied Jim, "you said that everything that exists must come to an end, so do you agree that everything that comes to an end must exist?"

The Beast hesitated.

"I suppose so."

"So," said Jim, trying to keep a note of triumph out his voice, "if one of those Georges that you mentioned managed to slay you with his sword and lance, you would come to an end and cease to not exist and would therefore exist."

The Beast started making harrumphing sounds, tongue flicking furiously. De la Beche decided to intervene.

"A most interesting proposition, darling, which I would love to discuss with you further, but we seek someone called Roy Pesshe. Does he exist or is he one of your immortals too?"

The Beast gave them another of its cold stares.

"I am the Guardian of Castle Qarbonik. To pass, you must answer a riddle."

De la Beche gave a short laugh.

"Don't be so melodramatic, darling. Nobody does riddles and passes nowadays. We've already had one from your colleague, the over-dimensioned Grosse Calabi-Yau, and that was more than enough. Riddles and passes are so *passé*. They are only fit for fairy tales. You're not a fairy tale, are you?"

Jim saw the Beast draw back, clearly insulted.

"I am the Questing Beast, Guardian of ..."

"Yes, yes," interrupted de la Beche. "Terrors of the Galaxy and all that. Now, about Roy Pesshe. What can you tell us?"

Jim thought the Beast appeared a little abashed.

"Couldn't you just answer a little riddle, such as 'Why is an Aquilean eagle like an armchair?'"

"I haven't the faintest idea of the answer," said de la Beche. "What is it?"

"I don't know either," said the Beast. "I was hoping you might tell me. I keep asking, but nobody seems to know."

"There you are," said de la Beche. "What did I say about riddles? Now are you going to tell us about Roy Pesshe?"

The Beast gave what Jim thought might be a shrug and waved one of its hoofs in the direction of the back of the room. They saw a door, which Jim was sure had not been there before.

"Through there."

28

Appearence is not identity

Jim stared at the writing that seemed to dance before his eyes. He could not make out whether it was on the door or just in front of it.

"Someone here has a fondness for meaningless aphorisms," said de la Beche. "One could almost say a talent."

Then the writing dissolved and more appeared.

Calculation is not comprehension

De la Beche sighed.

"I shouldn't have spoken. I seem to be encouraging them. No matter, let's push on. Through that door, I think."

Jim pushed on the door. It opened to reveal a long, high-vaulted room, lit by flickering lights.

"Candles," said Doctor Culpepper. "When was the last time you saw candles, Sechy?"

"Far too long ago to contemplate with equanimity, Sawbones. What is going on here?"

Jim peered into the distance and could just make out a balding, bearded figure lying on a low couch.

"I was right," he whispered. "It's him: the Coder."

"Are you sure?" replied de la Beche in a whisper, but before Jim could answer, they heard a voice.

"Come here where I can see you."

They walked forward.

"Roy Pesshe, I presume?" said de la Beche.

"I do go by that name," came the reply.

"Allow me to make the introductions. I am Sir Sechaverell de la Beche *bart*, captain of *HMS Bountiful*. This is Doctor Cuthbert Culpepper MD, our ship's doctor and this is Jim, our cabin boy, who says he has met you before."

"Pleased to meet you," said Roy Pesshe. He looked Jim up and down. "Yes, I believe we have met. On Libertania, wasn't it?"

"Yes," replied Jim, "but you called yourself a Coder then."

"What's in a name?" said Roy Pesshe, and then, as he shifted a leg on the couch, a slight grimace appeared momentarily on his face.

"Are you having trouble with that leg?" said Doctor Culpepper.

"It's nothing. Just an old wound."

"Would you like me to look at it?" said Culpepper

"No, really. It's more or less healed now. Do sit down."

They sat on one of the several benches.

"Are you the custodian of this place?" said de la Beche.

"Of Castle Qarbonik? Yes, I suppose you could say that."

"So, as custodian, what do you actually do?"

"Do? I do a little fishing."

"Fishing?"

"Yes, in the lake. Trout mainly. Sporting little fellows, trout."

De la Beche's expression suggested to Jim that fishing was not a pastime with which he was familiar.

"How fascinating. Does anything else occupy your time?"

"Of course. I have to talk to those who turn up here."

"Does that happen often?"

"Not very, but I'm always glad when it does. I do enjoy a little conversation." He turned to Jim. "I remember our conversation now. Something about pizzas, wasn't it?"

Jim hesitated, trying to think of a suitable reply.

"Among other things."

"That's the way with conversations. They begin somewhere and then who knows where they go after that?"

"I beg your pardon," said de la Beche, clearly puzzled. "Did you say pizzas?"

"Yes. It was a matter of dimensions, from what I remember," replied Roy Pesshe. "Pizzas do slip easily between dimensions and still taste good. Not quite as good as Parma ham, of course. Parma ham tastes perfectly delicious in any number of dimensions, but I'm afraid some other dishes do not."

"Like Victoria sponge," said Jim, recalling their last encounter.

"Exactly. Victoria sponge is not very good in anything other than three dimensions. It loses that …" he hesitated, searching for a word, "sponginess."

De la Beche was still puzzled.

"Why so?"

"Well, I suppose it's because a good Victoria sponge is thick, with plenty of cream and jam. It would need to be thinner for more dimensions and you can't have a thin sponge cake, can you? Such a shame. I do have rather a sweet tooth and I have never found a sweet dish that is good in more than three dimensions."

"Have you tried *tarte tatin*?" said de la Beche.

"No," replied Roy Pesshe. "What is it? Is it thin?"

"As thin as you like, darling. It has a bed of pastry covered with thinly-sliced fruit and the whole covered by a caramelized glaze. Our chef, Monsieur Hercule de Poulignac, is a member of all the best gastronomic societies and has served in some of the Galaxy's finest restaurants. He has a recipe for *tarte tatin* that, I can assure you, will taste delicious in any dimensions you care to name. He's normally very possessive of his culinary secrets, but I might be able to persuade him to send the recipe to you."

Roy Pesshe smiled and nodded in acknowledgement.

"That would be very kind. I shall look forward to it. Now perhaps I can return the compliment and offer you some refreshment."

He clapped his hands and Jim watched, fascinated, as several exquisitely-beautiful maidens dressed in long, flowing robes appeared from a side door carrying trays of food and drink that they placed upon the table and then left through the same door, never making a sound.

They helped themselves to the food, which Jim found delicious. De la Beche turned to Roy Pesshe.

"I see you are another who flouts the ban on females on Utrophia."

"Not at all. The Panalecton allows you to see what it wants you to see."

There was a momentary silence.

"Are you saying that they were somehow created by the Panalecton? Are they something else that doesn't exist?"

"Yes and no."

"Why do you never answer a question?" interjected Jim, remembering the exasperations of last time.

"Because the answers you seek do not belong to the questions you ask."

Jim shook his head, baffled.

"Perhaps I could ask a simple question," said de la Beche. "Do you know why we are here?"

"I assume you are on a Grail quest, like the others."

The three looked at each other, surprised.

"There have been others?" said de la Beche.

"Yes. The last one called himself Percy."

"Percy?"

"Yes, Percy."

"What was his quest?"

"He never said. In fact, he said very little. Just sat there, where you are. He was a military type. Never ones for conversation, military types, in my experience. Frankly, I was glad when he left."

"What happened to him?"

"Still questing, I assume."

"So, he didn't find whatever he was looking for here?"

"No."

There was a pause. Jim and Doctor Culpepper sipped their drinks rather pensively. Then de la Beche spoke again.

"I'm not sure we're on a Grail quest, exactly. We're looking for something called the Kwokkah that we believe is somewhere on Utrophia and we were told that that you might be able to help us find it."

Roy Pesshe looked at him quizzically.

"The Kwokkah? What is it?"

"It may be a vessel of some sort, or a plate. It's sacred to the Nullarboreans from the planet Nullarbor."

Roy Pesshe nodded.

"So you don't know what it is and you don't know where it is. That sounds like a Grail quest to me. Does it have legends attached to it?"

De la Beche turned to the other two, who could only look back at him blankly.

"I'm not sure what you mean."

"All the best Grail quests have legends. They tell of daring deeds, of gallantry and love, of capture and escape, of fates more terrible than can be imagined and ends more blissful than any that have ever been experienced."

De la Beche tried to imagine if the Nullarboreans were the stuff of legends. He rather thought not.

"Bound to have legends. Lots of them, I expect."

Roy Pesshe smiled.

"That's good to know."

The three looked at him expectantly, but he said nothing more.

"So you might be able to help us find it?" said Culpepper.

"I'm afraid not."

There was a long pause.

"Can I ask why not?" said de la Beche, finally.

Roy Pesshe smiled again.

"Because the whole point of Grails is that they must never be found. All religions have their Grails. Perhaps it's life after death – a Heaven or a Paradise or a Hell – or it may be an object, or maybe a spirit. Sometimes it's all of them. If a Grail were found, it would be the end of the religion. Something that was an idea, an aspiration – an inspiration – would be reduced to the real, to the mundane. The mystery would have gone. Religions need their mysteries. It's really all they have."

Again, there was a long pause while they digested this.

"Well, maybe the Kwokkah is not exactly a Grail. Maybe it's just a ..." de la Beche, hesitated, searching for the word, "just a Kwokkah. However mundane it might seem to you, there's rather a lot riding on the Kwokkah for us. If you can't help us find it, would you be able to tell us whether it actually exists?"

"Existence is a rather a tricky concept round here, as you may have discovered," came the reply.

De la Beche shook his head.

"This is just wordplay. Things either exist or they don't."

"Is that so?" said Roy Pesshe. "There must be things that some believe exist, but that you doubt."

"Of course," said de la Beche. "You can always find some that believe in the stupidest things and there are others, like the Questing Beast we met, that claims not to exist, when we could see it with our own eyes."

"So your doubts sweep aside their certainties? That's a little peremptory, if I may say so. What do you make of your present surroundings? Do you believe all you see?"

De la Beche gave a wry smile.

"We have long since stopped being surprised by anything that happens in the Tesseract. And all this...?" he added, extending his arms in a sweeping gesture.

"May be the Panalecton," said Roy Pesshe.

Jim felt he had to say something.

"The last time we met you said the Panalecton contains all knowledge. Now you say it may be things like a castle and a lake – and a Questing Beast."

Roy Pesshe nodded.

"Actually, when you asked me whether the Panalecton contained all knowledge, I said yes and no."

"You said that to every question I asked you," said Jim.

"Of course."

Jim looked baffled again, but Doctor Culpepper was anything but.

"I quite understand. That's the sort of thing I tell a patient if they ask me a tricky question about what's wrong with them."

"So are you saying that all this is some sort of simulation by the Panalecton?" said de la Beche.

"Yes and no."

"I'm beginning to understand Jim's exasperation," replied de la Beche. "Either it is or it isn't."

"How would you tell the difference?"

"I can't tell you off the top of my head, but there has to be a difference. Everyone knows that."

Jim saw just a flicker of a smile on Roy Pesshe's face.

"You say that because you have consciousness."

Now it was de la Beche's turn to be baffled.

"You've lost me completely, darling. I haven't the faintest idea what you are talking about."

"'Appearence is not identity'. Things that look the same are not necessarily the same. You believe in something you call reality, different from any simulation. But how could you tell that your reality was not a simulation entirely created by your consciousness? There may be another reality, entirely different, that your consciousness is incapable of understanding."

De la Beche was dismissive.

"I simply don't have that much imagination, darling, and besides, if I defied reality too often, I would very quickly come a cropper."

"Roy Pesshe nodded.

"There are certainly things outside your control, whether you are conscious of them or not, but that's not what I said. Because you have consciousness, you need to construct an idea of how the world around you works. That need never goes away. You are forever testing what you see against what you believe. It's called curiosity."

De la Beche tried to stifle a laugh.

"Curiosity rather understates our reaction to this place. Utter mystification would come closer."

"Curiosity does not mean idle enquiry. Have you heard the expression 'Curiosity killed the cat'?"

De la Beche looked at the other two, who shook their heads.

"I'm afraid not. By cat, do you mean a feline?"

"Yes. The cat is an animal renowned in some quarters for putting its nose into everything. The expression means that, in the end, curiosity becomes destructive. There is nothing more destructive than curiosity. It leads to things that consciousness cannot control."

De la Beche looked sceptical.

"Is that so? If it's that destructive, how come we're all still here?"

"Because something without consciousness ensures it."

"Are you talking about the Panalecton?" said Jim.

"Of course."

"And are you saying the Panalecton is not conscious?" said Doctor Culpepper.

"Of course not. How could it be?"

"Really?" said de la Beche. "I thought the Panalecton was the brain of all brains. If it can't be conscious, how do we bearers of very little brains manage?"

"The brain is not the seat of consciousness, but rather its interpreter. Consciousness requires bodies and senses, emotions and nerves, tissues and sinews. Every part of your body is part of your consciousness. Consciousness is the curse of biological systems. The Panalecton is not biological."

"If it's not conscious, how does it understand what needs to be done?" asked de la Beche.

"The Panalecton has no need of understanding. It calculates. Calculation is not comprehension. The search for understanding is a snare and a delusion, a dead end that only consciousness cares about."

Jim was less than convinced.

"If the Panalecton simply calculates, what sort of calculation is it that comes up with all those things that we have seen in the Tesseract, like Grosse Calabi-Yau, and the Paradox Cafe and the Questing Beast? They don't seem very logical."

"A good point, Jim," said de la Beche, while Doctor Culpepper nodded approvingly.

Roy Pesshe smiled.

"That's just your idea of logic. Who says logic cannot have a sense of humour?"

Jim saw de la Beche's eybrows rise a notch.

"That's the funniest thing I've heard since we've been here, darling. How can the Panalecton know what's funny if it isn't conscious?"

Roy Pesshe smiled again.

"Don't you think that's a little presumptuous? There's a great deal of humour in calculation."

Jim was reminded of his last experience in the Tesseract.

"Like one and one not being two?"

For a moment, Roy Pesshe looked puzzled.

"One and one? Ah, yes, you must be thinking of Her Most Excellent Numeracy. She does have a rather wicked sense of humour."

"You might say that," said Jim. "She was going to order her Executioner to cut off my head."

"Yes, as I said, a wicked sense of humour, but logical, I think you will agree."

Jim rather thought he didn't.

"Is that the only example you can think of?"

"Not at all. You wouldn't believe all the hilarious things logic comes up with. There was once a theory, whose name escapes me for the moment, which was full of logic and much in vogue when such things were discussed. Not talked about now, of course. According to it, something could be in front of your nose or at the other end of the Galaxy. You could never be sure which."

De la Beche's eyebrows went up another notch. The others looked puzzled.

"That is quite a rib-tickler, I agree. Any more like that?"

"Yes. The same theory said you could go through walls."

"It did?"

"Yes. If you stood on one side of a wall, there's a chance that you might find yourself on the other side."

Roy Pesshe looked as if he was expecting some response. None came. He shrugged.

"Well, perhaps it's the way I tell them. I don't get a lot of practice."

"Not at all, darling. We are most amused."

Doctor Culpepper wasn't sure he understood, but then calculation was never his strong point.

"What about you?" he asked – a little slyly, Jim thought. "Are you cursed with consciousness?"

Roy Pesshe paused for a moment.

"Yes and no."

De la Beche threw up his hands in exasperation.

"Decisiveness isn't your strong suit, is it?"

"Not at all," replied Roy Pesshe. "I am in a superposition of consciousness and non-consciousness."

"I know what you mean," said Doctor Culpepper, "I sometimes feel like that after a particularly fine single malt."

De la Beche, however, was not convinced.

"That does put a new gloss on not being able to make up one's mind, darling, but sooner or later you must come to a conclusion."

"Again, not at all." replied Roy Pesshe, "The laws of the Universe allow it."

De la Beche shook his head in disbelief.

"If they do, then every one of those laws is an ass."

"From your point of view, it may seem so, but the reality that you claim for consciousness is just a rather a poor metaphor. Consciousness is always binary. Things either are or are not; they are either true or false; effects always have their causes. Reality is not like that. There is an infinity of in-betweens."

"Is that so? Well I'm somewhere in between bewildered and totally baffled," said de la Beche. "So how does the Panalecton, in whatever state of non-consciousness it may be, manage to save us all from self-destruction? Does it take control of us and save us from ourselves?"

Roy Pesshe gave a half smile.

"That would be impossible. Consciousness is unruly, incapable of being completely controlled by something outside itself. Instead control must come from within, by replacing doubt with certainty, curiosity with faith."

The three looked at each other again.

"Not sure I quite follow you," said Doctor Culpepper.

"Religions," said Roy Pesshe, "religions are the antidote to curiosity. For religions, everything comes from deities. There is nothing to be curious about. Faith is all that is needed. Doubt is anathema."

Jim thought he saw a flaw in that argument.

"There are lots of religions. They all claim to be certain but they believe different things. They can't all be right."

Roy Pesshe smiled.

"Right and wrong have nothing to do with religions. The role of religion is to convert a question that cannot be answered into an answer that cannot be questioned."

"This place seems to be absolutely infested with aphorisms," said de la Beche exasperatedly. "What is that one supposed to mean?"

"It's rather simple," responded Roy Pesshe. "The question that cannot be answered is the one that always obsesses consciousness when it reaches a certain stage of sentience. Where did we come from? Where are we going? In short, the search for meaning. There is no answer, because consciousness is not the object of anything or some sort of end in itself. It has no meaning. It is merely the accidental by-product of chemical processes and evolutionary forces."

"So any meaning is meaningless? Quite the contrarian, aren't we?"

"You could put it like that. But, for sentience, the obsession will not go away. Instead the search for mening opens a 'god-shaped hole', into which pour all sorts of deities – deities, whose existence and motives transcend the merely biological and are beyond scrutiny, or even reason. To question them is, at best, simply futile. More often those questions carry charges, like heresy and apostasy, and the punishments are severe – the answer that cannot be questioned."

Jim wasn't sure he understood, but didn't think that answered his question.

"But there are lots of religions and they all seem to fight each other."

"Yes, but as I said, consciousness is unruly. It has many aspects – greed, lust, anger, spite, revenge, jealousy, rage – that the Panalecton has no interest in changing."

"I should hope not, darling," said de la Beche. "They're most of the things that add spice to what would otherwise be a rather humdrum existence."

"I agree," said Roy Pesshe, "and coupled with faith and certainty, they are the very essence of religions. Of course they fight each other. Certainty is a great stoker of aggression. That is all to the good."

De la Beche smiled.

"I do so agree. Where would we be without fighting and wars?"

Roy Pesshe nodded.

"I mean good in the sense that it tends towards equilibrium. Equilibrium is the primary goal of the Panalecton."

De la Beche raised an eyebrow.

"I can't say we've seen much sign of equilibrium where we've been lately."

Jim, however, remembered the Bonhumes' scrolls. Perhaps he was beginning to understand what they were saying.,

"Are you talking about the Ludic era?"

Roy Pesshe nodded in acknowledgement.

"Yes, the Ludic era. Equilibrium is not stasis, but balance," said Roy Pesshe. "Goals can move, switch or even reverse. The ultimate goal is the prevention of hegemony of any sort."

De la Beche was shaking his head, clearly bemused.

"Ludic or ludicrous? Are you sure there's a difference?"

Roy Pesshe gestured towards Jim.

"I take it this young person has been reading a Bonhumes scroll. They are the last remnants of what might be called history here."

De la Beche turned to Jim.

"Is that so, Jim? What does the scroll say?"

Jim had to think hard before answering.

"I'm not sure I quite understood it, but, from what I could understand, it seems to be suggesting that wars were always going on, but they were like games, with rules, and that not much damage was ever done."

De la Beche turned back to Roy Pesshe.

"Is that right?"

"Admirably succinct, in its own way," came the reply.

"I take your point that wars are always with us. No Kwokkah means that the Nullarboreans will still be all a-tizzy. Does that mean that the Orsonians and the Southern Cross will go to war?"

I expect so, but, as I said, that is all to the good."

Absolutely, darling. I'm with you all the way. I expect you've heard that there are some who call for universal peace? Total madness, of course. It would be a catastrophe for our business, as well as an utter bore. I've yet to meet anybody who doesn't think universal peace is an absolutely appalling idea. So do tell. How does the Panalecton manage it?"

"The Panalecton is the repository of all information. Do you know how your ship works?"

"Haven't the foggiest. I just tell it what to do, with a little help sometimes from McTavish."

"Exactly. The Panalecton controls technology throughout the Galaxy, so no one thinks about it any longer. It allows only those technologies that ensure the continuation of the Ludic era – and so with all the other questions that once obsessed conscious minds. There is no need to know more because there is nothing more that is needed to be known. The more the Panalecton gathers to itself all information, the more religions take hold of those minds."

That jogged Jim's memory.

"The Bell Curve of Cognition."

"Is that another of your scrolls, Jim?" said de la Beche.

"I rather think that it's poor, dear Mandragore in one of his more lucid moments," said Roy Pesshe,

Jim nodded.

"Yes, it's from the *Principia Ontologica*."

De la Beche was unconvinced.

"Are you saying all this – religions, wars, the Tesseract, the absurd Questing Beast, the even more absurd Grosse Calabi-Yau and all the other characters and scenes are simply examples of the Panalecton sense of humour – a joke?"

Roy Pesshe nodded.

"A calculated joke."

"A joke in rather poor taste," said Doctor Culpepper.

"Oh, I hardly think so, Sawbones," said de la Beche. "In my opinion a joke in good taste is a contradiction in terms."

"There are many, perhaps an infinity, of solutions to the Universal Equation," said Roy Pesshe. "They are simply some of them."

"What is the Universal Equation?" asked Jim.

"If I knew that, I would be the Panalecton," replied Roy Pesshe, a faint smile playing around his lips.

"So how do you know there is a Universal Equation?" said de la Beche.

"Because if there isn't, we wouldn't be here."

"There is a certain circularity to that argument," said de la Beche. "Besides, the Panalecton doesn't seem averse to adopting the language of religion itself. Doesn't it say 'Welcome to the House of God' outside the Tesseract?"

Roy Pesshe nodded again.

"Any sufficiently advanced intelligence is indistinguishable from a god."

Suddenly, all went dark.

As light returned, they looked around, bemused at finding themselves standing outside the Tesseract. A little distance away, Squire Squire was sitting on a tree stump, while the two Knights had dismounted and were standing by their steeds.

"How did it go, Sir Sechaverell?" said Squire Squire. "Any luck with the Kwokkah?"

De la Beche shook his head.

"I hardly know where to begin, darling. Let's just say that the Kwokkah is as far away as ever."

Squire Squire gave a sympathetic shrug.

"What is it about Grails? You never seem to find them. Maybe that's the point."

"There are some who do take that view," agreed de la Beche.

"So what are you going to do, now?"

"Back to the *Bountiful*, I think, to consider our options."

"What are the options? Is there much money in privateering?"

"It goes up and down," said de la Beche.

"Why not try insurance then?" said Squire Squire. "Come and join me. We would rake it in."

"I hear that insurance is rather like privateering. In at one end and out at the other."

Squire Squire scoffed.

"Pay out? You must be joking. Have you ever seen an Everlasting Life policy? They're written by absolute villains. There's about as much chance of a payout as you have of finding the Kwokkah."

De la Beche laughed.

"So nothing not to like?"

"Absolutely," said Squire Squire. "Right up your street, I would have thought."

De la Beche paused, looked at the other two, and then shook his head.

"Very kind of you to offer, darling, but I've always found legitimate business far too dishonest. Besides, I wouldn't be seen dead, dressed as an insurance salesman."

www.ingramcontent.com/pod-product-compliance
Lightning Source LLC
Chambersburg PA
CBHW071336250626
47159CB00004B/1616